Corbit-Calloway Memorial Library
Odessa, Delaware

D0108369

Natural History

Natural History

History

A NOVEL BY

Joan Perucho

TRANSLATED FROM THE CATALAN
BY DAVID H. ROSENTHAL

ALFRED A. KNOPF
NEW YORK 1988

THIS IS A BORZOI BOOK
PUBLISHED BY ALFRED A. KNOPF, INC.

Copyright © 1988 by David H. Rosenthal
All rights reserved under International and Pan-American
Copyright Conventions. Published in the United States by
Alfred A. Knopf, Inc., New York, and simultaneously in
Canada by Random House of Canada Limited, Toronto.
Distributed by Random House, Inc., New York.
Originally published in Catalan in Spain as *Les histories naturals*
by Edicions Destino, Barcelona in 1960.
Copyright © 1960 by Joan Perucho.

Library of Congress Cataloging-in-Publication Data
Perucho, Joan [date]
Natural history.
Translation of: Les històries naturals.
I. Title.
PC3941.P47H513   1988   849'.9354   87-46295
ISBN 0-394-57058-8

Manufactured in the United States of America
FIRST AMERICAN EDITION

Having contemplated this phenomenon, I must confess that although I deem myself brave, before facing such a being I would commend my soul to God.

—*In Praise of Thrashings,*
BARTOLOMÉ JOSÉ GALLARDO

But now that our noble Queen Isabella II has come of age, a new era has dawned, relegating our past to the realm of history.

—*Memoirs,* DON MANUEL LLAUDER,
MARQUIS OF THE VALLE DE RIBAS

"One day in a café in London," said Monsieur Decremps, "I ran into a short Breton named Kuffel whom I had known at school. After exchanging the usual pleasantries, I asked what he was doing in that country. He replied that he spent almost all his time at the Academy. 'My warmest congratulations!' I exclaimed. 'How I wish I were so lucky!'"

—*Encyclopedia on Method*

Contents

Contents

Translator's Foreword

JOAN PERUCHO has long been considered one of Catalonia's most engaging and original novelists. Born in Barcelona in 1920, he spent his formative years under the Spanish Republic. During this period (from 1931 to 1939), Catalonia was autonomous and its citizens free to speak, write, and study their own language. With Franco's victory in 1939, however, the public world of Catalan letters collapsed. Books were burned and their publishers shut down, while offices were hung with signs reading *No ladres; habla el idioma del imperio* (Don't bark; speak the imperial language—i.e. Spanish).

As a consequence, Perucho's first book (*Beneath Blood*, 1947) was printed secretly, as was the literary magazine (*Ariel*) that he helped to edit between 1946 and 1951. Not only the Catalan language but all experimental literature was illegal in postwar Spain. At the same time, Perucho entered the judiciary, where he remained until his recent retirement. At first obliged to keep his literary activities under his hat, he was gradually able, with the softening of the fascists' oppressive policies, to emerge from the literary underground and openly claim his rightful place as an author. Perucho's writings include verse (his *Collected Poems* appeared in 1984), art criticism (e.g. *Culture and the Visual Arts* and *Joan Miró and Catalonia*), essays on the pleasures of the table (he is a member in good standing of the National Academy of Gastronomy), and—especially—novels. Among these, perhaps the most popular is *Natural History*.

Natural History recounts the adventures of a dashing and

aristocratic young naturalist, Antoni de Montpalau. We first meet Antoni in a Barcelona convulsed—like all Spain in the 1830s—by the First Carlist War, a struggle between liberals and constitutionalists aligned with the regent Maria Cristina and her daughter Isabella II, on the one hand, and Catholic reactionaries and absolutists devoted to the pretender Charles V on the other. In Catalonia, the liberals' center of power was the coast, including Barcelona, while the Carlists (those favoring Charles V) were strongest in the mountainous interior, for example around Berga in the north and Morella in the south. Antoni, whose sympathies as a man of science lie with the liberals, soon finds himself traveling deep into Carlist territory in search of a vampire who has terrorized the village of Pratdip. He frees the village, seals the vampire's tomb, and is betrothed to Agnès, a local damsel as valiant as she is fair. But the vampire himself eludes our hero and journeys north, disguised as a Carlist guerrilla leader known as the Owl. Antoni, his coachman Amadeu, and his cousin Isidre de Novau then set out in search of the Owl. Before they can venture very far, however, they are captured by Carlist troops under General Cabrera, who turns out himself to be among the vampire's victims.

Despite their opposing political views, Montpalau and Cabrera become close friends. While the constitutionalist forces (under General Espartero) close in on Cabrera, he and Montpalau try to track down the Owl. Their quest is urgent, for only if the vampire is destroyed in Cabrera's lifetime can he avoid joining the ranks of the undead. After several near-misses, they finally locate and annihilate their foe. Simultaneously, Cabrera and his troops are defeated by Espartero and forced into exile. Antoni and his beloved Agnès are reunited upon his return to Barcelona.

Natural History is partly the chronicle of Antoni de Montpalau's education. Beginning as a facile positivist, he discovers (as Perucho notes in his index) "poetry through three things: love, mystery, and adventure." His appreciation of adventure is strengthened by his intimacy with Cabrera, who, while Montpalau uses his scientific skills to heal him, schools his young friend in such millennial virtues as dignity and nobility. Their parting at the end of the war is one of the book's high points:

> "I can never repay you!" Cabrera exclaimed. "I know neither what fate holds in store for me nor where I shall be tomorrow, nor do I know what will become of this wretched land of ours. But whatever happens and wherever I may go, do not forget that I consider you my brother."
>
> Then he removed his saber and handed it to Montpalau, who remained silent.
>
> "Take this saber as a token of my esteem. As you can see, I have nothing else to offer and it is my most prized possession. Take it."
>
> "Thank you, general," Montpalau replied, looking away to hide his tears.
>
> Gripping the young naturalist's arm, Cabrera muttered, "You're a damn good liberal." And smiling, he added, "The only one I ever met."

As in Perucho's other novels, myth, history, and the author's exuberant fantasies constantly color one another. For example, King James of Aragon really did take Princess Yolande of Hungary as his second wife, but Duchess Meczyr and Graetz Castle are the author's inventions. Together, these elements draw us into Perucho's vision of a Catalonia deep in memories, alive with the resonances of past eras and personalities conjured into being by his poetic imagination.

To see *Natural History* and its author in proper perspective, the American reader may find some general background useful. Catalan is spoken by approximately seven million people, some of whom live in the Balearic Islands, others in a small strip of southern France that includes Perpinyà (Perpignan) and others in Spain proper, from Alacant (Alicante) to the French border and between the Mediterranean Sea and Aragon. A Romance tongue, Catalan is closer to Provençal and Italian than to Castilian (the language usually called "Spanish").

The most interesting Catalan literature is of two periods: from the late Middle Ages through the early Renaissance, and from around 1870 to the present. The first era produced such outstanding writers as the Valencian lyric poet Ausiàs March (c. 1397–1459) and the novelist Joanot Martorell (c. 1410–1468), whose masterpiece *Tirant lo Blanc* was praised by Cervantes as "the best book of its kind in the world." During the past hundred years, Catalonia has produced an astonishing body of artistic work. In the visual arts, the genius of figures like Salvador Dalí, Antoni Gaudí, Juli Gonzàlez, Arístides Maillol, Joan Miró, and Antoni Tàpies is universally recognized. Catalan writing is of equally high quality, but the world has been slower to become aware of its virtues—partly because of a lack of good translations, and partly because of the Franco government's deliberate suppression.

Since Franco's death, Catalans have moved steadily toward self-government. They now have their own chief executive and Statute of Autonomy. Catalan predominates in the schools, and Catalan daily newspapers, television channels, and radio stations are free to operate. Thanks to novelists like Perucho and Mercè Rodoreda and poets like J.V. Foix and Salvador Espriu, Catalan literature remains as vital as ever. Its vitality has everything to do with the mixture of whimsy and inspired yarn-spinning, of artistic experimentation and love for the Mediterranean's past and people, that we find so brilliantly realized in *Natural History*.

DAVID H. ROSENTHAL

PART
ONE

The Naturalist

THE light streaming through the panes took on the purple, blue, yellow, and red hues of the geometric forms filtering it. It cut obliquely through the air till it glittered in the eye of a monstrous *Scolopendra martirialis*. Outside, the courtyard's slender columns rose, nearly strangled by thick vines and framing a botanical garden whose every plant and bush was neatly labeled. Sometimes, when a breeze arose, you could hear a vegetative rustle, gentle and suggestive, mixed with the sound of pieces of cardboard flapping against each other. Then the robot, animated by some suddenly released spring, vainly sought to strum its guitar and silently moved its lips. They had left it on the gallery some time ago, when the craze for recreational contraptions had ended, replacing it with a new machine for stamping calico.

The eye bulged in its socket. The iris glowed in the penumbra, but every day, at the same time when the light struck it, that glass ball became hard and precise, taking on a malignant and obsessive significance. It reflected the silk tapestries covering the gold damask on the walls, with their damp spots, a bit mildewed through the passage of time, and the carpet from Bangkok, a present from the Archduke of Austria, just as he fled Barcelona on the eve of the great catastrophe. Farther away, the eye struggled to follow the graceful frozen flight of an *Aurea picuda*, gallantly adorned with flashing colors. Or it pondered the moth-eaten fur on a *Simius saltarinus* bought from Yehuda, a Jew in the ghetto, by Jaume Salvador, the great naturalist who had begun, moved by his love of learning, to cunningly circumvent the Holy Office's restrictions. The eye paid special attention to an *Otorrinus fantasticus*, a small yet ferocious beast that shot lethal quills like poisoned darts. It came from Asia. Far beyond the eye, out of its range, there were cabinets labeled "macabre" with shrunken human remains: heads, ears, lips bizarrely disassociated from any facial structure, vague suggestions of phallic protuberances, all with the repulsive feeling of a living organism. They came from the jungles of South America. The eye grew still more savage as it lit upon the limp *Tenies intestinalis*, which, submerged in an indefinable yellowish liquid that filled some glass jars, swayed calmly and rhythmically at the slightest trepidation. When there was a full moon, a shadow fell upon the gallery's panes and, inexplicably, entered the museum's great hall, moving toward those visceral shapes.

Almost weightless, a delicate chandelier hung from the ceiling. On the walls, one could see portraits by unknown artists of Linnaeus, Arnau de Vilanova, Jaume Salvador in his youth, Sir Lammarck-Boucher et de la Truanderie, and also his relative Antoni de Montpalau, a Barcelonan nobleman, the owner of an excellent natural history collection and the palace in which it was housed. Montpalau's arrogance, position, and sweet words troubled the dreams of the city's marriageable aristocratic damsels. In one corner of the room, right above a little bookcase stuffed with folios and manuscripts, the Chamber of Commerce declared Antoni de Montpalau i de la Truanderie an honored member of that worthy and learned society.

He coughed discreetly, as though excusing himself. Then, with graceful steps, he strolled amid the specimens, stopping to observe some detail. He made for the door and stepped out into the entrance hall. Having reached the steps, he glanced at the *Courreur des Sciences* and also looked through the window at a fragment of the graceful *Aurea picuda*. The grooms, having turned the carriage around, had hitched up the horses, and Amadeu the coachman waited respectfully beside its open door.

It had been a splendid idea, very much in keeping with his notion of progress, to install that platform so the carriage, freed of its horses, could be turned in the small yard and thus be ready to depart immediately.

He thanked Amadeu and said, "No, I'd rather stretch my legs a bit."

At that moment, he was puzzling over whether the *Avutarda geminis* should be classified as a mammal. Jaume Salvador, in his wisdom, had left the matter unresolved, and at the committee meeting last Wednesday there had been a notable lack of consensus. Perhaps he should consult Madoz y Fontaneda in Seville, who was in touch with American naturalists. Who knows? Only experimentation could settle the matter. Without a real *Avutarda geminis* on hand, nothing could be determined. Otherwise, only hypotheses or—as his elderly colleagues put it—fantasies were possible. One had to use reason and scientific observation. Yes, that evening he would write to Madoz y Fontaneda, known as "The Divine."

Crossing Lledó Street and Saint Just Square, he plunged into a labyrinth of capriciously twisting lanes. From time to time he had to flatten himself against a wall to let a carriage pass or avoid dripping baskets carried by fishmongers, who threaded their way through the crowd balancing their wares on their heads.

He continued till he reached the site of the new street Count Charles of Spain had dedicated years before to the foul memory of King Ferdinand VII. He stood there for a while, looking at the houses being torn down while others rose in their places. He thought that, in the future, he should consider possible advances in construction, for it was obvious that the builders' routines and especially their methods had not changed since the Roman Empire.

He emerged in the Pla del Teatre, where clusters of peasants and shopkeepers discussed new developments in the Carlist War. There were blind men selling broadsides, while women with breasts bursting from their bodices offered cheap portraits of

General Mina and colored lithographs of his stomach devoured by cancer.

It was almost midday. The sun caressed the facades and the cobbles on the Rambla de Santa Mònica. The sky was a limpid, transparent blue. Making a supreme effort, the *Aurea picuda* struggled to intone its enchanting song in homage to Montpalau, but the acoustics were unfavorable and the townsfolk, apart from popular political ditties, wished only to hear airs from *La Fattuc-chiera* by Vicenç Cuyàs, a lad of twenty-one who had breathed his last just as his opera was being wildly applauded at the Teatre Principal.

He stood there for a moment, gloomily pondering. He recalled reading somewhere that those favored by the gods always die young. But the spectacle, even *in mente*, of a composer cut down in his youth depressed him. He managed to steer his thoughts toward the subject he loved best and decided that a long and arduous path lay ahead before that species could be satisfactorily classified. If the country at least had a stable government and if partisans of the old regime weren't still battling to impose reaction and intolerance! He was overcome by a sudden wave of liberal enthusiasm.

He had reached the "Flea Bastion." Outside the Customhouse Barracks across the street, troops maneuvered and he could see from their aspect and the heavy guard around them that something was amiss. The soldiers' uniforms were red and blue, with white bandoleers and tall hats. Every other day there was some revolt or disturbance, execution or assassination. The country was in an uproar. There were still ruins and charred buildings from the last riot. The rabble sang:

> "Six bulls were in the bullring.
> None was any good.
> That's why they burned the convents
> In my neighborhood."

The Naturalist

He leaned against the wall and gazed out at the calm sea. There were six vessels, one of which flew the Union Jack. A screeching *Gavinis communis* cut across his field of vision. Silence fell. Up above him on Montjuïc, the Spanish flag fluttered. Some riveting but inaudible, entirely nonexistent chords sounded. Colonel Riego's image appeared, his anthem, the 1812 Constitution. You could see Carlists, the Citadel, and Colonel O'Donnell falling upon the flagstones, bleeding slowly and absurdly. His blood oozed onto the stones. Militiamen passed, singing patriotic songs, and people shouted "Long live the queen!" A *Gavinis communis* and an *Avutarda geminis* flew by, in the latter case of undetermined species, screeching and flapping above Xifré's new city gates. You could smell salt spray, and delirious optimism alternated with the blackest despair. Everyone flapped and screeched. Only science remained impassive, beyond good and evil. Only science, exorcising shadows and ignorance, reducing them to light and progress. Some shadows, however, seemed irreducible: shadows from mountain gorges, still unformed but awaiting a propitious moment to materialize. At times, livid and spectral, they flickered beyond the panes or took the forms of fluttering bats.

He turned and brushed the elbows on his frock coat. Then he set off toward the Pla del Palau. Shots occasionally could be heard far away. Up in Gràcia, a thick, black column of smoke rose, a prelude to liberty or ignominy. A volley rang out a moment later.

A finch flew by and landed on the rim of a fountain. It drank rapidly, with amusing little pecks. Then it took a few hops and preened its feathers with its beak. He noticed it staring at him.

At that moment, he only had ears for the *Aurea picuda*'s song. It was harmonious and ineffable, something like human brotherhood or love of knowledge, and it came from the heavens or the Enchanted Isles.

When he opened his eyes, the finch had disappeared.

The Carnivore

THE masks are either black or red. The waists are pinched by corsets, though sometimes these are unnecessary. A smile appears behind an opaline goblet. The walls are lined with huge mirrors, mirrors that let you glimpse a terrified neck's youthful elegance, a head bending over a *billet d'amour*, or a waxed mustache. The grand duet is just beginning, a great, passionate scene of hopeless love, with Italian ruins as a backdrop, stolen kisses, languid gazes, gloves forgotten in stage boxes. It could end in pistol shots and red roses on starched shirt fronts. But that's uncommon. Barcelona's high society, though aristocratic, is provincial. Better to think about vessels, ship chandlers on the Ribera, gold from the Indies, and the first mechanized factories. There's a long tradition of captains and pilots. Four hundred nautical days, neither more nor less. On the facades, you can see multicolored signal flags, forming a rosy cloud around a compass, hardtack, rigging, salt cod, names of ships like *The Polar Star*, brand-new logs, and letters home. Workers arrive at five A.M., bringing their lunches with them and tromping through the deserted streets. Apprentices sleep on counters and slave away, taking measurements and talking up the merchandise. They only go out on Sundays, each with a penny in his pocket, and they have to be back in time for evening prayers. It's true that there are also clergy, officers, and men of learning. Majestically, they play the cathedral organ and organize slow processions with burning candles, brass bands, and associations, including the Academy of Science and the university, recently returned from Cervera.

The air shuddered. A burst of devilish laughter and sulfurous breath shattered the kaleidoscope brought especially from Palermo, the land of optics. Tiny ghostly figures danced among the splintered glass, leapt over obstacles, and vanished in the distance. The alpha and omega sign appeared.

Antoni de Montpalau did up a button on his silk vest from Lyons, a present from a cousin on his mother's side, the Baroness of Néziers. Picking up a piece of rock crystal between two fingers and peering at it against the light, he told Novau, "Really, I'm tremendously interested in whether the *Avutarda geminis* is a mammal. It's a strange phenomenon. There is a precedent, of course, in the *Vampiris diminutus*, commonly known as the bat. There are many curious and notable legends about this little beast, especially in the Balkans, concerning its unproven ability to suck human blood."

Novau, a seasoned sea captain, felt a trifle uneasy. He was still aware of the immobility, quite impertinent and disconcerting, of that *Scolopendra martirialis*'s eye. It was as though within its retina a dreadful jungle scene shuddered. He spat.

They were sitting in the botanical garden. The air smelled fresh and sweet, and the light was pale green. From that corner they could see the robot, frozen in some inexplicable gesticulation, and also the textile machine, a little rusted by the rain.

"The *Avutarda geminis* comes from South America," Antoni de Montpalau continued. "According to our not entirely reliable information, it has remarkable curative powers in cases of gallstones, diarrhea, and enlarged spleen. The second vertebra in its tail, counting down from the appendix, when soaked in reduced mandrake juice also possesses virtues that I am obliged to doubt without experimental evidence. A Valencian uncle of my friend Arnulf de Viladode once claimed that, being in Pernambuco on Maundy Thursday and with the bishop's permission, he witnessed a mass cure of certain blacks suffering from malaria, which would not be especially interesting were it not for the fact that the local medicine man also made use of the *Avutarda geminis*'s healing powers. Naturally, as you will understand, I have no faith in such old wives' tales and my purpose is to disprove these fantastic legends."

At this moment, they felt a strange vibration that seemed to come from a nearby tree whose foliage was exceptionally dense and luxuriant. Its branches began to sway and droop as the vibration grew more violent. Novau leapt from his cane chair.

"It's feeding time," our gentleman calmly announced. "It's an unusual species of carnivorous tree. Don't be alarmed. It was a great effort to acclimatize it here. Winckelmann, one of Germany's outstanding naturalists, wrote me a while ago that His Majesty's Royal Academy would pay ten ounces of gold for a small cutting."

As he uttered these words, Antoni de Montpalau gracefully clapped his hands and Silveri, the footman in charge of the plants, appeared. He was carrying a big cage full of sewer rats, all squeaking furiously.

Silveri opened the cage at a slight distance from the trunk and cautiously stepped back. The rats staggered forth, stupefied by the vibrations, and the voracious branches immediately closed over them. Not one escaped. The tree slowly resumed its original posture and, having digested the rats, opened its leaves, from which some small skeletons the color of old ivory tumbled.

Silence fell. Pavanes could be heard, coming from the Bonaplatas' palace next door and delicately played by Ramonet, their eldest son, who had gotten the chambermaid Pepeta pregnant. She had been packed off to their farm in Sarrià, where she had died giving birth.

It was an atmosphere of perfect beatitude. The carnivore let itself be soothed by the breeze and the gentle melodies. Everything took on a timeless air.

Novau tried to rouse himself and yawned. Isidre Novau i

Campalans was, as we have mentioned, a highly competent sea captain, though rather taciturn. Related to the Montpalaus, he came from an illustrious lineage that, like our hero's, had sided in those troubled times with the archduke's party. As a child, he had lived for long periods with his great-aunt in Lloret, where his love of seafaring had been born. He had studied navigation in Barcelona and Cádiz and had often sailed the Caribbean. Before winning the title and post of captain, he had survived three shipwrecks in which he had been on the point of bidding his great-aunt farewell forever. As he stood watch one day during a run to Malta, he caught a glimpse—not granted to many—of Niccolò, the *pesce cola* so dreaded by the Genoese. Upon rising the next morning and looking in the mirror, he saw that at least half his hair had turned white as snow, greatly improving his appearance. He was now staying at his cousin Antoni de Montpalau's home in Barcelona, where he hoped to cure himself of a disease caused by protracted lack of fresh food.

"Tomorrow, dear cousin," said Antoni de Montpalau, "we'll visit our farm in Gràcia. And in passing, we'll determine the state of liberal opinion and see how they fare in that celebrated town."

He seemed about to add something, but he uttered not another word. Beyond the carnivore, amid the courtyard's arches, a shadow slowly moved. He thought his eyesight must not be quite right. Now it had disappeared.

The two gentlemen strolled among the phanerogams. From time to time, they plucked a sweet pea and sniffed its fragrance. It was almost time for lunch.

When they left the botanical garden and entered the dining room, they were struck by an intense sulfurous smell. Antoni de Montpalau saw the fragments of his kaleidoscope on the carpet. He stood there for a moment, lost in thought.

Behind its mask, black or red, the shadow let out a macabre laugh that slowly dissipated in the air.

The Liberty Café

G RÀCIA is a town with an intensely democratic tradition that, years later, would be symbolically em-
bodied in its famous tower and the weekly that bore its name.
The Marquis de Sallent, in his memoirs, describes the progressive,
hard-working town as an unbreachable bastion of liberty. "One
native of Gràcia," he declares, "inflamed by his convictions, with
a weapon in his hand and his back to the wall, will suffice to rout
all the sinister forces of reaction and their loathsome hordes."
The Marquis de Sallent died in a Carlist ambush near Campdevànol, battling like a lion. *The Young Observer*, published by
the Junta of Berga, declared that with his death, the constitutionalists had lost one of their most vicious captains and congratulated both itself and His Majesty Charles V on their glorious
victory.

It was a splendid day. Montpalau and his cousin set out from
Barcelona that morning. The air was mild, and everything looked
crisp and clear.

They had settled into the carriage. Novau held a polished
mahogany box inlaid with gold initials. He deposited it carefully
on the luggage rack.

"Pistols," he announced. Montpalau said nothing and merely
nodded. Nonetheless, he thought his cousin was overdoing it.

They rode through New Gate, driving among irrigated
fields. The horses broke into a cheerful trot and Amadeu, the
coachman, felt so gay that he couldn't keep from humming
under his breath.

The fields stretched away on both sides, and an occasional golden farmhouse rose up before them, large and majestic, with geraniums in its windows. They breathed in the sweet country air; everyone felt happy.

As they neared Gràcia, they saw some militiamen breakfasting beneath an arbor beside the road. A large bottle of wine with a long spout sat before them on the table. One of them motioned Amadeu to halt. He examined the captain general's safe-conduct and then let them pass.

They reached Gràcia without further incident. Swept along by the horses, they rumbled through the town, making a terrific racket, and emerged on the other side, heading for a hill where the Montpalaus had for many generations owned a farm called Partridge House. The house itself was large, with drawings incised in its facade and a huge sun dial at the top with a large but pedestrian motto: "I live with the sun."

They were welcomed by the peasant's wife, who came out wiping her hands on her apron and acting delighted to see them. A few dogs sniffed at the gentlemen's feet and then indifferently retired.

Montpalau invited his cousin into the house. The inside was cool, and everything was submerged in a pleasant penumbra. The woman opened the windows and drew back the heavy old drapes. Some immense rooms then appeared, with console tables and bureaus upon which bell jars rested, full of coral, tiny seashells, and faded ribbons. Time had settled, with a gentle sound like impalpable ash, upon the furniture, upon portraits of uncles and cousins smiling frozenly through the years, recalling hunts and lost shotguns, disconcerting stares and yellowed letters, the birth of an heir and the fires of civil war in rustic hamlets. Time settled there in tenuous strata, silently superimposed, turning colors and winter evenings gray. It swept through the empty rooms, sedimenting every surface, countless cracks and crevices in furniture and curtains, with memory's ashes.

After taking a turn through the deserted chambers, Montpalau spoke to Isidre, the peasant, about changes in his crops and handed him some instructions the Chamber of Commerce had printed concerning the introduction of new agricultural methods. They argued over every detail and observation, but at last our gentleman vanquished the peasant's irrational resistance, attached as he was to outmoded and uneconomical practices. The Chamber of Commerce's pamphlet bore the title: *Historical-Critical-Practical Instructions or Memorandum to Encourage Agricultural Progress through Fertilization.*

Meanwhile, Novau had tried out some methodical-ambulatory exercises in the fields and now gazed pensively at a large holding tank overflowing with little frogs. When his cousin called him, he put his pipe in his pocket and waved. He felt inexplicably happy and free.

Then the two gentlemen, in shirtsleeves and aided by Isidre and six farmhands, energetically harvested half a ton of medicinal plants specially grown on the property, including citron, sorrel, cardamom, and cloves. Montpalau planned to send them as a gift to his friend, Doctor Samsó Corbella, in the hope that they might prove useful in his efforts to find a cure for Pott's disease.

They lunched in the large dining room, where they enjoyed some excellent dishes: meatball soup, thrushes with olive sauce, hare *aux fines herbes,* and pig's feet with young turnips. For dessert, they barely touched a basket of delicious green plums and, after lighting two Cuban cigars of deep and velvety aroma, they looked out at Barcelona and the sea.

They said goodbye to Isidre and his wife. Montpalau told Amadeu to take them back to Gràcia, to the Liberty Café. Once again, they clattered through the streets and stopped outside number four, El Carrer de la Virtut.

The Liberty Café was a slightly dingy establishment. The town's most exalted elements could usually be found there, making speeches and signing passionate manifestoes. The walls were dark red, and in the middle of three of them, framed by oval garlands, allegorical representations of Industry, Commerce, and

Navigation were painted, personified by ladies whose soft, rosy flesh was modestly draped in fluttering veils. All of them rendered homage to a still more august lady who smiled at them from the wall facing the door: Liberty. Pondered, uttered, chewed over, belched, and quaffed, she tightrope-walked above the customers' heads. She cheerfully greeted them. With a delicate hand, she inscribed her high-sounding, heroic name: Liberty.

The place was crammed to the rafters. Blue cigar smoke rose, lending the room a divelike aspect. Among the newspapers devoured and discussed were *The Steamship, The National Guard, Uproar,* and *The Constitutionalist.* This last periodical's masthead was graced by the following verses:

> I'm a democrat through and through
> With nothing left to lose.
> When I can raise my head again
> I'll take no more abuse.

The two cousins ordered coffee. Montpalau glanced about him and eavesdropped on the conversations. From time to time, however, his thoughts wandered to the *Aurea picuda* and the mystery of that rare and wonderful bird. He struggled to hear its elusive song.

A man wrapped in a long, black cape entered. He stood by the bar, downing a couple of brandies. Then he turned and took a few steps toward Antoni de Montpalau. It all happened in a flash. He flung open his cape and fired a pistol. Our hero barely had time to duck instinctively.

Chaos ensued. Fright occasioned by the shot gave way to furious indignation. Novau leapt at the assailant, who, taking advantage of the pandemonium, swiftly dodged between the tables. By the time Novau reached the door, the assassin had vanished.

Montpalau stood up, pale as a ghost. He was immediately surrounded by a solicitous, angry crowd.

An ethereal lady approached him. Transparent, winged, pondered, uttered, written, and dreamt, she stood at the victim's side with a voice like an *Avutarda geminis*, soothing as a baby mammal's. She spun through space, through the universe in Liberty's and Justice's state of grace. They were Progress's two cogged wheels, striking fear into the hearts of livid, spectral shadows with fanatical eyes and scarred, unshaven faces— especially malignant mountain shadows that descended toward visceral forms.

Fortunately, the attack had failed. Montpalau, helped by his cousin and Amadeu, climbed into the carriage. In the street, groups of bystanders railed against the reactionaries. A poultry seller offered Montpalau, with maternal insistence, a tender chicken from Prat that would make a comforting soup.

"Poor guy," she said. "They scared him half to death." And her face twisted in a grimace meant to be dreadful and condemning.

Anxious and shaken, they set off for home. The sun hung low in the red, translucent, terrifyingly unreal sky. They could hear distant croaking that seemed to float in the air.

From time to time they drove through a cloud of mosquitoes. High grass grew by the roadside. Some mules ambled along, with tinkling bells around their necks.

Novau silently lit his pipe. Antoni de Montpalau sat lost in thought. A pothole made the carriage tilt perilously. Silence fell.

Turning a corner, they spied Barcelona's lights.

4

Theory of the Dip

O N his doctor Samsó Corbella's orders, Antoni de
Montpalau spent the next day in bed. It was a preventive measure. Corbella recommended moral and physical rest
during exactly twenty-four hours. Propped up against some
pillows, our gentleman could contemplate the botanical garden,
since his bedroom on the second floor looked out upon the courtyard. The day was wet and overcast, with intermittent thunder-
storms. Water trickled onto the gallery's small red tiles, which
glistened as though they had just been waxed.

Faithful Novau kept him company and, at his request, read
from various books. In order to see the expression on his face,
Montpalau asked him to fetch some non-nautical treatise—for
example, the mysterious anonymous medieval *Treatise on Geniture* that our hero had discovered quite by accident in a peasant's
attic. Following Montpalau's instructions, the intrepid captain
looked for the manuscript and, after carefully but vigorously
dusting it off, he began at random: "The Dip hath a malevolent
nature and containeth many natures and loveth deathe, from
which he liveth. And when he wisheth to enter some playce to
worke hys will, he treadeth very light and cunningly, and if he
heareth hys feet make a noise he raiseth them off the grounde by
enchauntment. And he hath another quality: that should he spy a
manne before the manne spyeth hym, that manne loseth all his
pow'r and he goeth strait for hys blood. And he hath yet another
quality: that hys neck hath such strengthe that he cannot turn
but turning hys entyr bodie as welle. He liveth only from blood

*1*7

and cannot abide the sighte of garlick, parslee, purslayne, crosses nor mirrors either. And he hath yet another quality: that as he willeth, he changeth into an ante, a bee, a spidre, a roostre, a wolfe, a wilde ass, a lobstre, a dogge, a vypre, a swanne, a lyon, a weasle, a larke, a cloude of damp nighte ayre, a tygre, a unicorne, a panther, a hyena, a peacock, a swifte, a hedgehogge, a crocodyle, a vypre, a pelicaune, a beavre, a woodpeckre, a stork, a falcon, a vultur, an eagle, a horse, a whale, a foxxe, a fenix, an elephaunt, or a parrot."

Novau stopped and looked inquiringly at his cousin. Montpalau remained silent, as though struggling with some enigma.

The rain had slackened. The wind, however, howled ominously down chimneys and around weathervanes on towers. It stripped the leaves from the trees, whisking them over convent walls toward deserted squares and narrow lanes with evocative names. It beat against windows with a clatter of broken panes, and whipped the hats off members of the National Militia. At times it halted couriers and caused stagecoaches to delay their departures with a thousand excuses. Such was the case outside the Four Nations Inn, where Ferdinand de Lesseps waited impatiently to set out for Manresa, in which city Baron de Meer maintained his headquarters. The French consul in Barcelona and a great friend of Montpalau's, Lesseps had begun to hatch a grand but hopelessly chimerical engineering project. He loved prints and voyages, and hanging on his bedroom wall he had six engravings much envied by Montpalau and bearing the following titles: *Marché aux poissons à Rotterdam*, *Vue du lac de Bienne*, *Interieur de la cathédrale de Moscou*, *Monuments egyptiens*, *Vue du chemin de fer de Little Falls à Utica*, and *Eglise de Froitskoy sur le canal Fontonka à Saint Pétersbourg*.

Meanwhile, the shadow on the landing had shifted to the right. Impalpable and deformed, it struggled to open the door to the room with the natural history collection. It slid silently, dulling reflections in mirrors and gilding and at times disappearing altogether. In their immobility, the graceful *Aurea picuda* and the *Simius saltarinus* seemed old and moth-eaten, marching toward their final decrepitude. The shadow flitted, and there were moments when, through some vague refractions, something like a fantastic lithograph appeared with the rainy image of a ruined castle. The castle stood amid high mountains and menacing clouds, above a minuscule village in a shady valley whose lush meadows had witnessed blood-curdling scenes. At the bottom one seemed to glimpse: *Vue d'une ville et d'un château-fort en ruines.*

A short, dry cough was heard. In another volume, Novau continued with a second unintelligible passage: "The presaunt geniture of the Dip, recounted and transcribed in the degree 42 poly as telleth the Argolic tables and estimated howres and owing to a lacke of specymens we hadde to rouse our spyrits so that, preceded bye the luminaries in the signe of Pisces and blessed with goode lucke, the exaltation at fynding myself againe in the sunlyght was quenched and bye mee set aparte, resigning myself to the gratest fortune that the Devyl derived from that same signe and in the presaunt geniture to beholde the same degree of skyll, albeit he be stable in the seconde phase and valiaunt for such potente ends as Crese Dosip wisely writeth in the Ptolemaic revolutions of ast. Iud. Planetae."

Novau's heart froze at this interminable and utterly incomprehensible series of observations. He sensed something wicked and—so to speak—Balkan. He tried to think of the sea, of the sea's clear waters, of foam around the prow of a vessel with billowing sails. He thought especially of icebergs, of their immaculate whiteness beneath Greenland's icy blasts. He went on reading: "To discourse briefly upon the knowne remedees that muste be swiftlee employed, I sae that at the tyme of infectioun, being the ascendant attacked by the aforesayd through witchcrafte and succeeded by the moone's quadriture and Venus's influence will befalle hym, nor wille he quickly escape therefrom certaine directiouns of greate importaunce, though in the seconde yeare he will go strait for hys blood."

There was a knock at the door. A servant entered, carefully balancing a large tray bearing hot chocolate and wafers. He set it down on a three-legged table decorated with marquetry and paintings of bucolic scenes. First, however, he had to remove some books and precision scales, which he deposited on top of a chest of drawers. He did everything with great delicacy and emphatic gestures. He was from Lleida, and his name was Ramon.

The two cousins dipped their wafers in the chocolate as the afternoon waned. Ramon lit some Saxon oil lamps and drew the heavy curtains.

After wiping his lips on a napkin, Antoni de Montpalau said, "As you will understand, dear cousin, such descriptions are mere wives' tales. What you have read refers to a strange being known as the Dip. But what is a dip? you may ask. Has anyone ever seen one? A supposed being who changes into a spider, a bumble-bee, a vulture, a horse, and then an elephant?"

He paused. He drank a sip of water that he had poured from a crystal decanter.

"No, dear friend. Today science strives to dispel such super-stitions, born in a time of ignorance and error. The scientific method is inexorable. I admit that there are still certain inexplic-able phenomena that one struggles to comprehend. But science, based on reason and experimentation, will have the last word, I assure you."

Our hero spoke with great vehemence. Novau thought he detected a note of self-doubt.

"I believe you," he replied. "I believe you, beloved cousin. Nonetheless, do not forget that you are speaking to a man who, among other things, has seen Niccolò, the *pesce cola.*"

The young naturalist made a gesture that seemed to imply that he considered his cousin's response inopportune.

"Bah, Novau! Don't make me laugh! What you saw was nothing more than a hallucination caused by excessive ingestion of canned food. We've discussed your condition with Doctor Samsó Corbella. It's an open-and-shut case."

The cousins went on talking. Meanwhile, with feline deftness, night descended on Barcelona.

The city was dark. Only an occasional lantern shed its feeble light.

The silence grew dense and opaque. Occasionally, you could hear the vague rumble of National Militia patrols, a deep, far-off blast from some detonation. Then calm returned.

The shadow made an effort and contracted, taking shape and growing denser. It was like an unfocused, blurry vision. For a few moments, one could feel the malevolent, obsessive, swirling vibration of something invisible slowly turning into tenuously illumined mist. This continued briefly and then dissipated.

Shortly thereafter, in inexplicably swift and sure flight, a bat or possibly an *Avutarda geminis* sped into the night's vastness.

The Diabolical Bull

PRINCE Felix Maria Lichnowsky, Count of Werden-
berg and Lord of Woschutz, whose heart beat, at the
age of twenty-three, with all the fervor of the absolutist cause
and who was an officer in Prussia's proud army, hastened to
offer his sword to the Spanish pretender Charles V when he rose
in the Basque provinces against Madrid's freethinking government. Brought up in the cultured atmosphere of Graetz Castle,
near Troppau, and the Palace of Kryzanowitz at Ratibor, heir to
one of the largest fortunes in Germany, the prince adored belles-
lettres. He also played the piccolo, an instrument much in vogue
at that time in royal courts, with consummate delicacy and
exquisite taste. He took part in King Charles's expedition to
Catalonia—which circumstance enabled him to meet and be-
friend the famous Ramon Cabrera, later Count of Morella. After
the above-mentioned expedition's failure, Lichnowsky joined
Count Charles of Spain's general staff and served as liaison between him and Cabrera, who operated on the other side of the
Ebre. This gave him a chance to explore the country inch by
inch and to learn the Catalan language, habitually spoken by the
era's two tigers: the one in Berga and the other in the Maestrat.
Lichnowsky, after the executions at Estella and Maroto's
treachery, remained loyal to the Carlist cause and continued the
hopeless struggle, sullied though it often was by Pep de l'Oli's
and Llarg de Copons's guerrilla bands. The prince, when not
leading his cavalry squadron, in which case he donned a blue

jacket and red beret and trousers, disguised himself in innumerable fashions—as a wagoner, a smuggler, a Ribera peasant, etc. His fame quickly spread, and people compared him—though their views were quite opposed—to the cunning liberal conspirator and man of action Aviraneta.

These events were broadcast and exhaustively discussed both in liberal newspapers and in *The Young Observer* of Berga, though naturally in quite contrary terms. That morning, Antoni de Montpalau had perused *The Constitutionalist*, which, after a violent attack on Prince Lichnowsky, had printed a patriotic ode by Joaquim Rubió i Ors, who signed his work "The Piper of the Llobregat." One stanza read:

> Of an ancient bard the long-muted lyre
> I shall snatch from his clammy tomb,
> And the muse who wanders sad by his grave
> I shall now with my song invoke,
> Awakening those who kindled glory's fire,
> Holy shades, valiant knighthood's perfume,
> Counts and monarchs in battle brave
> I shall in fame and beauty cloak.

Upon reading these verses, Montpalau nostalgically recalled his teenage friend and mentor, the poet Eudald de Puig, whose career had been cut short by his tragic death. They had met one day at a literary gathering at Cordelles School, shortly before it was shut down and when the poet was at the peak of his powers. The headmaster, Father Narcís Riera, had introduced them. Montpalau remembered Riera's generous praise of the Noble Royal and Imperial School of Cordelles: "The gentlemen who attend this school will enjoy not only its support and protection but also its example, stirring their gallant hearts to spurn idleness and childish pastimes unworthy of their births and to heroically embark on the study of great words and deeds, lest they sully the radiant honor of their alma mater. I shall never consign myself to the shadows some desire for their work, for there are none in this luminous and resplendent house whose arms include the sun's inextinguishable rays. Promise me, above all, much light, much favor, and the refuge and protection that all men require."

Setting aside these memories, our young naturalist then retired to his study, where he was preparing a catalogue of his herbarium with pen-and-ink drawings. He worked at it all morning, and felt positively satisfied.

That afternoon, since it was Sunday, the two cousins decided to head for the bullring, where the Italian Captain Cantalupo was going to ascend in an aerostat. Leaving their carriage near the customhouse, they made their way on foot through Barceloneta's thronged streets. People squeezed together on rooftops and beaches, hoping to behold the spectacle for free.

There were signs at the entrance announcing the program and prices: two pennies for seats in the sun, three for seats in the shade. In the middle of the ring, some men inflated the balloon while Captain Cantalupo, in a dress suit, strutted about giving orders. After tipping the chief guard, our friends made themselves comfortable in their front-row seats. The place was jammed.

At five o'clock sharp, to ascertain which way the wind was blowing, Cantalupo released some small balloons of assorted shapes and colors—fish, human beings, frogs, etc.—and once the aerostat was full, he bowed to the public and leapt into the wicker basket. The crowd's excitement was at its peak.

A brass band struck up a jaunty march. The aerostat slowly rose, while the spectators screamed and clapped. Some sandbags hung from the sides of the basket. When Captain Cantalupo had risen some fifty yards, he untied a few of them and flung a cloud of red, yellow, and blue leaflets down into the ring. They landed everywhere as the crowd ran to grab them. Montpalau stood up and caught a red one in his hat. The title read "To Barcelona," and beneath it were these verses:

Swiftly galloping, our wind-blown aeronaut
A lovely city beneath him doth chart.
A divine excitement he kindleth in his heart
Lending impetuous wings to his thought.
Blessed aspirations, happiness sweet
Exalt and inspire him as he recognizeth
The florid aroma that gently riseth
From a fragrant garden, love's very seat.
To swim amid light and, since God willed it so,
To see above him the sky, with Paradise below.

The aerostat went on rising, growing smaller and drifting toward Horta. The crowd gaped in astonishment, and bets were placed on where it would land.

The second part of the program included an unwonted event that made a lasting impression upon our hero.

Three bulls had been announced and were eagerly awaited, since they would provide a perfect conclusion, given the setting. As Antoni de Montpalau felt no attraction whatever to such grisly sports, he wished to leave but was won over by Novau, who wanted to watch the *corrida* and observe the mob's reactions. Being a good naturalist, Montpalau was repelled by gratuitous bloodshed.

The first bull came forth and, after the customary rites, it was slain and dragged from the arena amid contradictory exclamations. The sky had gradually clouded over and assumed a menacing aspect. Suddenly, a mysterious shadow appeared above the ring and descended in a bizarrely oscillating movement.

Then a bull black as night charged furiously into the ring. It stood there for a moment, panting before the spectators' fascinated stares. Then it turned, as though seeking someone or something. It took a few steps and, unexpectedly, ran toward our friends, leapt over the wooden barrier, and, rearing up on its hind legs, glared at Antoni de Montpalau. Two fiery eyes were fixed upon our hero's.

Everyone held his breath. The mysterious shadow thickened. One could hear the bull's heavy breathing. The devil's dark presence was obvious to all. The alpha and omega sign appeared.

Suddenly the diabolical beast took a leap and disappeared. No one knew how or whither it had fled. Breathless, red-faced guards combed every passageway. A great uproar arose, and people feared a repetition of the regrettable events of 1835.

These inexplicable occurrences were attributed to bad organization. On the morrow, *The Commercial Echo* published a harsh attack on the authorities, asking how, in an era of progress, such catastrophes could take place. It was truly lamentable.

Parisian Airs

THE theory of perfumes is vast and complex. To master it, one needs long experience and a certain voluptuous sensuality. A good perfumer must possess—among other things—taste, cultural refinement, agile intelligence, an elegant and assiduous manner with ladies, lively instincts, and a well-bred and precise sense of smell. With such baggage, one may attempt to discriminate among perfumes, grasping their exact and elusive nuances and noting their defects and impurities. As everyone knows, rare is the perfume whose nature is simple and straightforward. A few, it is true, can quickly be identified; but others, after a delicate sniff, require a degree of spiritual concentration that is attained with difficulty and then only by blocking out the world and closing one's eyes. These, the most problematical, are infinitely varied. One could, however, divide them into two broad categories: cool and warm. Among the former, suggestive of shade and freshness, one will happily recall those that embody—if it may be expressed thus—the sea or mountains, a grove, or simple trees and bushes with intimate connotations: lavender, rosemary, or even pine. The warm ones are associated with certain persons, especially females, and are condemned by preachers and ecclesiastics in general, who find them overly erotic and stimulating. One drop of such a perfume on a lace handkerchief can provoke devastating tempests in the hearts of the lovelorn. Like a butterfly, this drop flies through the air, unattainable and cruel, swiftly precipitating misfortune and tears.

Misfortune and tears. Prince Lichnowsky, bivouacked on the outskirts of Vimbodí, sniffed a perfumed silk handkerchief and abandoned himself to a state of emotional disorder brought on by the thought of a certain fair lady. She was framed by an oval medallion that also held a lock of her hair. From time to time a horse whinnied, and the prince stopped to listen. Then the lady returned, like a delicately floating pavane, like that perfume or a tear on a handkerchief. *La belle nuit d'amour.* This suggestive name had been devised by Monsieur de Vendres, the Baron of Néziers's perfumer; and the lady had acquired it with demure hesitation that had only been vanquished by the sight of another lady, elegant and fair, purchasing a bottle without the slightest embarrassment. As a result of this encounter, they became close friends, but the lady framed by the medallion was trapped in Paris, subject to her brutal husband's tyranny, while the other set out for Barcelona, where she and a famous musician planned to embark for the enchanted isle of Majorca. Her name was Aurore Dupin, but she signed her books—for she was a well-known author—with the refined though ambiguous pseudonym "George Sand." The famous musician, who composed extraordinarily sensitive sonatas, was called, as everyone knows, Frederic Chopin.

Antoni de Montpalau read all this two days before their arrival in a letter from his cousin, the Baroness of Néziers. He repeated the news at one of the Marquis de la Gralla's gettogethers, where it caused a sensation. After extensive debate, they resolved not to be overly scandalized by the couple's unusual situation, since Barcelona rarely harbored such illustrious guests. They all agreed, therefore, to welcome the travelers with all the honors they deserved. The Marquis de la Gralla informed his friends that he would organize a scientific-artistic gathering at his palace, where he hoped he could rely on their brilliant participation and especially that of his son Josep Ignasi, who would unveil his latest disconcerting invention: the pneumatic harp.

Everyone applauded enthusiastically. Antoni de Montpalau was chosen to reserve a hotel room, since, inasmuch as the visitors were unmarried, no one could lodge them at his home or lend an official character to the event. He thought the Four Nations Inn was the most suitable and up-to-date, though Barcelona's hotels in general were rather unsatisfactory at that time. Francesc Avinyó i Barba, the medical scholar who also manufactured calico prints in Poble Nou, said he would pay for some refreshments at the Peru Café.

Antoni de Montpalau, after consulting Ferdinand de Lesseps, who because of his position preferred to remain on the sidelines, reserved a room and also arranged certain exquisite details that would surely please the two travelers' delicate sensibilities. With Novau's help, he visited all the ships that sailed for Majorca and made a list of those that seemed most comfortable and seaworthy.

Mademoiselle Dupin and Frederic Chopin arrived in Barcelona amid a cloud of dust, having caught the Mataró stagecoach at Arenys de Mar. Meanwhile, Prince Lichnowsky, with his cavalry squadron, plotted an especially dastardly and dangerous attack on one of the government's convoys to the besieged town of Solsona; and the *Aurea picuda*, of ineffable song, found a grove of cork trees that made a perfect nesting-place, far from men's prying and treacherous eyes. There it intoned its inaudible melodies.

Antoni de Montpalau stepped forward and bowed deeply. Bells tinkled in the distance, along with Pyrenean chamois and lights flickering like lost moths, all spinning to the rhythm of a pianola.

The eagerly awaited couple descended, showing their pleasure at the unexpected welcome. They were immediately taken to the Four Nations Inn.

The Baroness of Néziers, in the cloud-enveloped villa she had named La Rochelle, smiled happily. Some salmon-colored clouds appeared, blown southward by the mistral. She sniffed a rose's fragrance and summoned Dentelle, her cocker spaniel, who was cynically raising a hind leg above a flower bed.

Hours later, in the Peru Café, the promised refreshment was served. Plates of caramel custard were accompanied by lady-fingers, almond cakes from Vendrell, cookies from Tortosa, and Valencian orgeat. Only Mademoiselle Dupin attended, for Chopin —she said—was a trifle indisposed. She was charmed by the group's cordiality and showed her appreciation of the orgeat.

"*C'est foutrement bon,*" she declared.

Her hosts froze, with their ladyfingers halfway to their lips. If they had understood her correctly, she had said something similar to the extremely unladylike Catalan word *fotre.*

Aurore Dupin was neither fair nor ugly, but she was certainly both chic and fascinating. Highly intelligent. Despite her unconventional vocabulary, she spoke with great refinement. Chopin, on the other hand, was tall, melancholy, and virtually silent. He greeted people, however, with great ceremony. They made a strange couple.

That evening, Antoni de Montpalau took a turn after supper to enjoy the cool night air. He wandered solitary through his neighborhood's streets, which always smelled of damp and filth. He could hear his footsteps echoing dully on the pavement.

He walked along, lost in thought. He felt slightly sad. A bronze bell solemnly tolled in a nearby steeple. He gazed at the sky and, after buttoning his frock coat, returned home.

A cat meowed despairingly.

7

The Pneumatic Harp

T H E Marquis de la Gralla threw a party worthy of his distinguished name. Apart from our hero and those special guests, the participants in his weekly gatherings were also present. These included Bartomeu Garriga, a sickly grammarian who had once met Jovellanos and who was currently working on toponymy. Because of some deformity, he always laughed out of one corner of his mouth. He usually smelled like apothecary's ointment and was not easy to get along with. Then came Segimon Ferrer, a remarkable mathematician who was writing a book entitled *Mathematical Origins of the World and Its Creatures.* He was constantly quarreling with another regular, Father Pasqual Matons, author of a liberal book of sermons that had caused him considerable difficulties with the reactionary Catholic censorship. Out of gratitude for his services to the liberal cause, the government had recently put forward his name for the bishopric of Murcia. *The Young Restorer,* another periodical published by the Junta of Berga (and controlled by his arch-enemy, Father Torrebadella), fiercely and pitilessly attacked Matons. Also present was Doctor Samsó Corbella, an eminent and highly erudite gentleman whose sole weakness was skirt-chasing—a fact that caused him some hair-raising conjugal scenes. Then there was Francesc Avinyó, one of Poble Nou's captains of industry, who had paid for their refreshments at the Peru Café. Avinyó was decisive, efficient, and innovative. And finally, one should mention Josep Ignasi, the marquis's eldest son, who at first glance appeared a bit mentally retarded but who had shown signs of uncommon mechanical and musical ingenuity. His latest invention was the pneumatic harp.

All these worthy members of the Marquis de la Gralla's circle found themselves gathered in his cavernous reception room, which was only opened on special occasions—for example, when General Llauder had summoned the city's leading lights to the marquis's house (a meeting that exasperated the extremist elements and was one reason for the assassination of General Bassa and Llauder's subsequent flight). The walls were adorned with gold damask, and large mirrors hung above big marble fireplaces. In a corner near a broad balcony that looked out upon the street, one could admire the moment's supreme musical novelty: the pianoforte, which was well on its way to supplanting the clavichord. At Josep Ignasi's suggestion, it had been ordered from Paris, specially packed, and the Pleyel company had sent a tuner to assemble it in Barcelona, wielding his fork in the palace for an entire excruciating week.

Seated on a sofa facing the pianoforte were the guests of honor, the marquis, Antoni de Montpalau, and Father Matons, who pretended he hadn't heard the story of Mademoiselle Dupin and Monsieur Chopin. The others sat in a circle around Doctor Samsó Corbella or stood about in small groups. From time to time, they approached the sofa and made polite conversation with the lady and her companion. After an animated discussion, and profiting from a moment's calm, the marquis signaled to Josep Ignasi while announcing that in honor of such a distinguished gathering and especially in homage to the famous artists he had the pleasure of seeing among them, his son, as he had already indicated, would play a few tunes on a pneumatic harp of his own invention, as he hoped to benefit from those illustrious friends' responses.

Some wigged footmen immediately entered bearing a litter on which, protected by a sheet, a large, deformed object could be seen. Sweating and straining, they lifted it up, placed it in the middle of the room, and stood there awaiting further orders. Then Josep Ignasi clapped his hands. The footmen, as though they had rehearsed the entire skit, unveiled the glittering pneumatic harp. In its basic structure, the machine resembled a normal harp, but with the difference that it was built into a large mahogany box equipped with some pedals from which a pipe of considerable dimensions rose. This pipe, in turn, branched out into smaller ones that vaguely recalled an organ. Each string on the harp corresponded to one of the pipes. All together, it was a most bizarre-looking contraption.

After bowing to the group, Josep Ignasi seated himself on a stool and placed his feet on the pedals. He began to pump them furiously, saying his first task was to expel the old air. And indeed, one heard a phenomenal sound of wind escaping through a thousand and one holes. Having concluded this operation, the Marquis de la Gralla's heir, still pumping, delicately positioned his hands on each side of the harp, gracefully leaned forward, and, at the right moment, began an inspired rendering of Bellini's aria "Casta diva"—without the chorus, naturally.

It was a solemn occasion. The machine produced a striking simultaneous double sound. Along with a kind of metallic vibration, one could make out the organ's somber and velvety tones. It was extraordinary.

The applause lasted a long time. Josep Ignasi modestly accepted Monsieur Chopin's congratulations and urged him to play one of his own compositions on the pianoforte. Chopin finally agreed—but not right away, as Segimon Ferrer was about to discourse on "The Mathematical Principle of Coagulation in the Origins of the Universe and the Earth in Particular." In a finely timbred voice and with great conviction, Ferrer examined the various existent mathematical coagulations, starting naturally with water and ending with an analysis of what he proposed to call "transmutational coagulation." Finally, to crown his argument about the mathematical principle of coagulation's generative action, he produced a learned citation from Job: *"Instar lactis me mulxisti, et instar casei coagulari permisisti."*

This quotation sparked off a theological-scientific response from Father Matons, who inquired about the exact meaning, in regard to the generative principle, of mathematical coagulation and who turned the discussion toward strictly religious issues, on which he could discourse with great brilliance and logic.

Meanwhile, the guests frequently visited the buffet, though on tiptoe lest they disturb the fascinating dialogue. They repeatedly expressed their admiring approval, while also chewing as quietly as they could.

The controversy ended happily, in that neither party entirely bested the other. The most varied and stimulating laudatory pyrotechnics then burst forth. Mademoiselle Dupin declared that the marquis had no cause to envy the salons of Paris, and she would even go so far as to say that they lacked the élan of his gathering. She spoke excitedly, especially with Samsó Corbella and Antoni de Montpalau, and was shocked when she heard of the latter's strange adventures: that is, the attempted murder in Gràcia and the diabolical bull's inexplicable behavior.

Antoni de Montpalau calmed the refined authoress, attributing his unusual experiences to the turmoil in the land. This seemed to cover the first incident; in regard to the second, Montpalau explained Abbot Poncet's theory of the influence of thunder and other atmospheric phenomena upon animals' nervous systems.

Someone called for silence. Finally, at the insistence of those present, Monsieur Chopin seated himself at the pianoforte.

He appeared pale and absorbed. He hesitated a few seconds. Then he began to play, seeming to caress the keys. An extraordinary music poured forth, whose existence no one had suspected until then. There was something poignant and light, with a deep, delicate, sublime melancholy. It was music of genius.

No one ever forgot the impression made by that music, so intimate and yet so grand. It was a seed, silently sprouting in their hearts. It conjured into being a world of latent emotions that only now broke through into conscious awareness.

On the morrow, Aurore Dupin and Frederic Chopin set sail for Palma de Majorca aboard *The Majorcan,* which belonged to Trullols. They left behind some true friends who would always remember them, as well as a touch of sadness. It was inevitable.

8

Natural History of Catalonia

F ATHER Pere Gil of Reus, who entered the Society
of Jesus at the age of twenty-three, wrote a monu-
mental *Treatise on the History or Natural Description of Those
Things Native to Catalonia* that remained in manuscript for many
years. At the request of the Royal Academy of Natural Sciences,
Montpalau was preparing an annotated edition. Aware of this
circumstance, Baron de Meer, who planned to construct several
fortresses, asked our hero for a petrographic report consisting of
those parts referring to stones and minerals. Montpalau sent him
chapter six, entitled "On the Variety, Nobility, Excellence and
Value of Catalonia's Stones, Both for Construction and for Other
Purposes and Effects; and on Certain Precious Stones Found in
Catalonia":

"Since Catalonia, as was mentioned in the preceding chapter,
is almost entirely or in its majority mountainous, it follows that it
offers abundant stone for building, and certain plains like Urgell,
Penedès, Vic, Cerdanya, etc., where no mountains can be found,
possess excellent soil for making tiles and are provided with stone
from nearby mountains, whereby handsome churches, public
buildings, houses, and towers are commonly found in Catalonia.
So much so that all the cities, of which there are eleven, and all
towns in which magistrates reside and all coastal towns and most
or virtually all Mediterranean villages and many other places
great and small possess splendid stone or brick walls with watchtowers, as will be discussed below in the second book. And since
from a certain species of heated stone lime and plaster are made,

and this type of stone abounds throughout Catalonia, also since Catalonia has much sand because of its rivers, streams, and sea-shore, it follows that buildings are both more solidly and more easily constructed in Catalonia than in many other Spanish and European provinces and kingdoms. Catalonia should thank God for her stones, as He created them, and despite the fact that the countryside around Tarragona and in other parts of Catalonia provides extremely hard stone for building, there is also sand-stone so soft that it can be cut with a metal saw and can be worked and smoothed so easily that stonecutters need only polish it."

At that moment, Antoni de Montpalau rose from his seat and, finding himself alone, furiously scratched his crotch. Then he continued: "In Montserrat, Girona, and many other spots, one finds very hard stone that can easily be polished and used in building. Girona in particular possesses abundant stone that resembles marble but is slightly darker. It can be polished very smooth and may be used in fonts, large and handsome altars, and other items of this sort.

"The stone quarried from Montjuïc, a mountain near Barce-lona, is famed throughout Catalonia. So much has been extracted without diminishing the mountain's size that many affirm that the stone grows, for otherwise this mountain would have either disappeared or shrunk. Montjuïc offers various grades of stone: Some are so soft that they could almost be sawed, but other varieties range from hard to extremely hard. All of it, however, can be cut and worked fairly easily. It is well suited to every sort of structure, such as city walls, battlements, bastions, churches, palaces, and private homes of rough stone whose win-dows, arches, and corners are of cut stone."

Our hero took the liberty of adding a critical note here, denying that Montjuïc could grow, at least in the manner im-plied by Gil, and citing the work of other eminent experts.

Then he continued his transcription: "A rock called 'black-stone,' found in the mountains around Tarragona, is very hard

but easy to cut and polish and is far superior to blackstone from
Girona. It resembles marble except for its color. Much of the
floor in Tarragona's cathedral is paved with this stone, which is
also found in certain chapels in the same cathedral: particularly
those of Don Antoni Agustí and Don Joan Teres, Archbishop of
Tarragona.

"Girona, as we have mentioned, possesses a sort of white
marble, but it is darker than the marble cut and polished near
Genoa. In the mountains by the monastery of Poblet, however,
extremely fine white marble is quarried that is little or scarcely
inferior to the Genoese.

"Jasper of assorted colors is quarried in the mountains
around Tarragona. And said jasper can be seen in certain columns
in Don Antoni Agustí's aforesaid chapel.

"But better jasper is quarried in the mountains near Tortosa;
such jasper is called brocaselle because it is streaked like brocatelle.
Many handsome columns and other objects have been fashioned
from this jasper, including a table and other items at the Catalan
Deputation's offices and in Don Antoni's chapel. Fine altar stones
are made from this jasper and shipped to many parts of Catalonia,
Spain, and Italy."

In the margin, Montpalau added another note on brocatelle,
the Catalan Deputation, and Don Antoni Agustí, who was related
to Baron de Meer on his mother's side. This also gave our
commentator a chance to praise the deputation's patriotism. It
was all mixed up with a bizarre episode involving Philip IV, his
partisans, and his opponents. Montpalau lit a cigar and continued.

"Alabaster is a white, translucent stone quarried in many
parts of Catalonia, especially in the mountains around Montblanc
and Poblet, though this variety is rather soft compared to the
alabaster near Sant Magí. This excellent stone is used in chapel
cornices and certain handsome sculpted images. It is also used in
windows, for carefully selected alabaster, cut very thin, admits
much light. Though the amount of light is not equal to what
one could obtain with glass, alabaster is safer and less costly, and

thus in the Reus Church and others in Tarragona and Catalonia one finds elegant alabaster windows, both stained and unstained, that admit much light and keep out more cold and wind than glass. Altar stones for very fine altars are made from alabaster. They have only one defect: Hard blows can more easily crack them than altar stones of jasper or marble, which are stronger."

This passage was followed by a description and study of rock crystals and precious stones like diamonds, emeralds, rubies, turquoises, amethysts, agates, etc., which Montpalau omitted in the belief that it would not interest Baron de Meer. Nonetheless, as he approached the end of this section, his eye fell upon a passage that made him start. It read: "Agates, which in Italian are called *corneline*, are commonly known in Catalonia as 'staunchbloods' because they will stop bleeding from the nose, mouth, or private parts. Splendid red agates are found in Catalonia near La Pobleta. One of their virtues is that they put vampires to flight."

A wicked cackle was heard. It was, as always, a sinister omen.

9

A Mysterious Letter

THE next day, Antoni de Montpalau received a hastily scribbled note from the Marquis de la Gralla urging him to come as soon as he could. It was a matter of great importance.

Our hero found the marquis in an extremely agitated state. He paced to and fro in his study. He was wearing a silk dressing gown whose stripes were the color of tobacco. Beholding Montpalau, he opened his arms and exclaimed, "At last, my dear friend! Please sit down, and thank you for coming so promptly! Something truly extraordinary has occurred. I've also summoned Samsó Corbella, Father Matons, Bartomeu Garriga, and Segimon Ferrer. If you don't mind, I'll wait till they arrive to tell you what it's all about. I think I'll feel a bit more comfortable that way."

Though his curiosity had been roused, Montpalau obeyed. Soon Ferrer, Garriga, and Corbella appeared. The last to arrive was the majestic priest, whom the marquis seated at his desk so he could preside over the proceedings. He was half-hidden, however, by a magnificent *Koeleria vilosa pers*, a species named after the eighteenth-century German botanist Georg Ludwig Koeler, author of *Descriptio graminium Galliae et Germaniae*. The canon moved his chair a little to the right and, with a clear view, sat back and prepared to listen. In fact, they were all on tenterhooks. The marquis, who had remained standing, enjoyed prolonging their anticipation. Finally he said:

"Dear friends, you all know that I have a sister, Baron

40

d'Urpí's widow, who lives with her daughter in an isolated mountain village surrounded by my former brother-in-law's vast estates. After the baron's death my sister, in a fit of mystical devotion to his memory, broke off all social relations and, leading the life of a recluse, spent nearly fifteen years, to the virtual exclusion of all other matters, performing works of charity and managing her properties. Indeed, for some time she had scarcely written to me, so distant had she grown from the world and its concerns. Before I forget, I should add that my sister lives in a village called Pratdip, not far from Mola de Falset."

Montpalau started. He asked, "What did you say?"

"Pratdip," replied the marquis, fixing Montpalau with a glance somewhere between severe and puzzled. Then he continued, "My sister had not written for over two years. Yesterday I received a missive that was no simple family letter full of domestic details and allusions that such letters normally contain but rather, dear gentlemen, a cry of anguish from a poor woman pleading for help, humbly and fearfully, against a peril both mysterious and—I would venture to add—supernatural, though my scientific convictions (begging Father Matons's pardon) forbid me to employ this adjective before conducting an investigation of the phenomenon *in situ*. Obviously, this letter greatly interests us as scientists, and I can affirm without the slightest reservation that if the facts recounted therein are true, then, beloved friends, Providence has deposited the affair of the century in our laps to the perpetual glory of Catalan science."

Having spoken thus, the marquis picked up a letter that lay among the papers on the table. He cleared his throat and read it slowly and emphatically:

"To Josep Martí i Llubra, Marquis de la Gralla
Dear brother,
    I know that, upon receiving this letter, you will wonder what prompts me to write after such long silence and that, although your heart is generous and loving, you may

well and deservedly reproach me before opening it. I apologize, dear brother, and, setting aside the reasons I might adduce but lack the strength to enumerate, I beg you to heed the voice of a poor tormented woman who, together with her daughter and this village's inhabitants, beseeches you, as a representative of science and learning—since the governmental authorities have proven utterly unavailing—as desperately as I may to succor those menaced by a dreadful danger.

For nearly a month now, we have lived in terror and apprehension. The villagers had always whispered about the Dip; but it was something so illogical, monstrous, and improbable that neither I nor my husband (may he rest in peace) ever paid them any notice. This strange being's origins are lost in the mists of time, and everyone speaks of him, at least to outsiders, as an evil legend. In people's minds, however, the true lord of this land was and still is the Dip, endowed with the capacity to survive the passing centuries and who, from time to time, appears out of nowhere to claim his blood rights. He only sallies forth by night because people say he is a corpse by day. No one knows, however, who or what the Dip is, for he possesses many natures: wolf, bat, scorpion, and God knows how many more. The sole remedy known hereabouts is purslane. but purslane quickly wilts and our supply is soon exhausted.

Excuse the incoherence of this letter. I truly fear that I shall go mad, for the Dip—or whoever he may be—has returned. Every morning we find a dead villager with the blood drained from his body and two small holes in his neck. Everyone, including the mayor, the constable, and Father Anton, lives in fear. "Whose turn will it be to-night?" we wonder despairingly. When I ask myself this question, as you may imagine, beloved brother, I especially think of my daughter, the niece whom you so often dandled upon your knee.

For the sake of your sister, who cared for you when you were young, for the memory of this child of whom you once were so fond, and above all for the love of Almighty God, come as quickly as you can, that the light of your intellect may illumine this mystery and deliver us therefrom.

> Your sister who implores you,
> Remei
> Baroness d'Urpí"

Having completed his reading, with tears in his eyes, the Marquis de la Gralla gazed around at his stunned and silent listeners. He said, "Well, gentlemen, I believe it's time to offer our opinions."

Segimon Ferrer, who greatly admired Voltaire, was surely about to make some impertinent remark to Matons, whom he glanced at nastily, but the philologist Bartomeu Garriga took the floor first.

"Just a moment," he said. "Before any of our illustrious colleagues offers his views on such exceptionally singular events, I believe that, possessing a certain knowledge of etymology and toponymy, I should first clarify the significance of this wicked personage's name. In fact, the term 'Dip' comes from Arabic, where it means 'savage being' and is frequently used in the sense of jackal, greedy for blood. The correct etymology of the name 'Pratdip,' therefore, would be 'Prat del Dip'—in other words, 'glen inhabited by the being whom we all seek to identify.' "

Breaking the ice of their initial astonishment, the philologist's statement set off a tumultuous controversy. Everyone trembled with excitement. They weighed the situation's ins and outs, speaking with grandiose gestures.

Antoni de Montpalau remained quiet and thoughtful, seated

in his chair. Suddenly he rose and called for silence. "Calm your-
selves, gentlemen. As a naturalist, I cannot accept the existence
of such diabolical beings, nor does the Church acknowledge
them. But we find ourselves faced with a case that science must
clarify. Let us behave, therefore, like scientists. We must not be
carried away by our emotions and preconceptions. We must
investigate, as always. We must coolly investigate. God has given
us a potent and matchless weapon: reason. We must use it to
explain what at first seems inexplicable. But that this may occur,
reason—or more exactly, science—must directly illumine the
phenomenon. We must go to that strange village and examine
the evidence so dramatically described. We must go to Pratdip."

Everyone applauded our hero's wise words. He was warmly
congratulated. The marquis said that, in reality, it was the only
sensible course of action and, since they could not all go as a
group, they should appoint someone they trusted. And as he
himself could not go, being related to the afflicted parties, and
virtually all the others were too old and infirm, they must ask
the only person in good health and also endowed with youth and
wisdom.

As the marquis spoke these words, those present fixed their
eyes upon Antoni de Montpalau. He again rose and, placing his
hand upon his heart, solemnly said, "I shall go to Pratdip."

Then our hero was embraced by his companions. A great
love of science and progress united them. Matons blessed him
with all the Church's maternal solicitude. Everyone felt satisfied.

In a grove of cork trees, the *Aurea picuda* again intoned its
silent and exquisite song.

10

Botany, Zoology, History

T H I S mandate from the Marquis de la Gralla's circle heightened Antoni de Montpalau's naturally acute sense of responsibility. Intending to prepare carefully for his expedition, he first tried to discover that mysterious village's exact whereabouts. He consulted detailed maps whose routes wound among high mountains and gorges and whose subreptitious rivers, of bizarre anfractuosity, flowed between banks covered with slippery lichen. He saw miniature nativity scenes and shadowy ravines, as though through a telescope, and imagined a sylvan beauty that seemed to have escaped from a book of prints.

He studied the native flora and fauna. He carried out deep and carefully pondered geological research. He learned about underground streams of sulfurous waters, calculating the quantity of their malign vapors and what influence they might have upon the inhabitants' psyches.

Beneath a bell jar, he slowed the flight of a *Vampiris dimi-nutus* and scrutinized the geometry of its circular trajectory as he could not have done, owing to its rapidity, in the open air. He was especially intrigued by this mammal, as it was linked in popular mythology with the final object of his study. Montpalau knew that folk beliefs, stripped of legend and fantasy, always have a solid basis. For this reason—though retaining his critical spirit—he prepared himself for every eventuality, poring over not only the famous *Treatise on Geniture* but Collin de Plancy's *Philinion* and Friar Calmet's *Dissertation sur les apparitions des*

45

anges, des démons et des esprits et sur les revenants et vampires, published by the Sorbonne.

He analyzed the Balkan legend according to which, just as underground streams influence the living, likewise buried corpses remain active in the outer world. Remnants of life keep the blood from coagulating and make the cheeks stay rosy, like two deathly flowers. In regard to effects upon the living, the defunct's capillary vessels develop an excess of energy. Life, which seemed to vegetate, reappears in all its vigor. The corpse, however, once in touch with its victim, produces a contrary effect just as a magnet polarizes iron. A nervous relationship is established at a distance. Since the vampire has not yet begun to decompose, the virus seeks an organism in harmonious correlation to which it may transmit its contagion. Just as buried metal and underground streams seek the light, so the undead seek, above all, to reestablish links with the living. Thus is a living man possessed by death.

Montpalau researched all these matters, racing against the clock since his intention was to set out immediately. He flung himself into a frenzy of activity, checking and piling up the most outlandish hypotheses as points of reference. Novau, who was very excited, told his cousin that he wished to join him in this adventure. The mountain air would do him good. Amadeu, the coachman, whom Montpalau had often forced to be a captive audience for his monologues and in whom he had inculcated a religious love of science, also showed his enthusiasm. He immediately told the cook that he would accompany his master, and she told all the other servants. That evening, as he gnawed on a chicken leg she had delicately offered him, he delightedly saw the deferential and admiring respect in their eyes. He had risen several rungs in the social hierarchy.

Last of all, our hero visited his friend Baron de Meer, the captain general. The baron, who had been apprised of the affair, gave him a special safe-conduct for all Catalonia. They had a long private chat in the captain's office. When they parted, de Meer wished his friend good luck.

46

As Montpalau left, he beheld a strange spectacle. Some Hungarian gypsies, dressed in gaudy and picturesque rags, were making a black bear and a goat with enormous twisted horns dance to the beat of a tambourine. The monotonous percussion had an enervating effect. A circle of onlookers watched the plantigrade's slow and graceless gyrations. Montpalau didn't know why, but he sensed that the fantastic goat was staring at him intently. It was a look he recognized.

Montpalau decided to set out as soon as possible—that is, the following morning—for Pratdip.

PART TWO

Monsieur Laborde's Itinerary

"ONE leaves Barcelona through Saint Anthony's Gate. After traversing some tilled fields, one turns inland, with the sea on the left, and sets out along a broad, straight highway lined by leafy trees through which one can glimpse various towns on either side: Sants, Sant Boi, Sarrià, Sant Just, and Esplugues. The traveler quickly passes through Hospitalet and reaches Sant Feliu, a populous town whose main street is flanked by handsome dwellings. Shortly after leaving Sant Feliu, one sights Molins de Rei on the right and arrives at an inn of the same name. Then one follows a short avenue lined with poplars till one reaches a bridge over the Llobregat. This recently built bridge is very solid, though inelegant, and has a pedestrian walk on either side. If the traveler continues down this avenue till it ends, he will see the road to Tarragona and Valencia on his left."

This description of the outskirts of Barcelona is taken from that great voyager Alexandre de Laborde's *Itinéraire descriptif de l'Espagne*, a work in which, after offering the reader a vision of the kingdom's various industries, the author makes a special recommendation: "*Il est nécessaire cependant,*" he says, "*d'être bien armé en voyageant en Espagne.*" The book enjoyed great success among Europe's educated classes, and in 1809 a second edition was printed.

The dust was of the highest quality. It filtered through every crack and crevice and stuck in our friends' throats. The young naturalist, accompanied by his cousin the frigate captain Isidre de Novau, was driven along at a terrific clip by his coachman,

Amadeu. This had only one drawback: that given the road's lamentable state, it made the coach rattle and jolt in a most disagreeable fashion. The travelers could scarcely speak because the shaking affected even their vocal cords and jaws, producing temporary stutters that frequently made their words unintelligible. Novau, who had assumed the role of quartermaster for the expedition, had followed Laborde's advice and packed not only the two customary pistols but also three magnificent, well-oiled, brand-new English rifles. Moreover, impressed by those Balkan legends about vampires, he had bought ten gross of small mirrors and pectoral crosses. He also planned, as soon as they reached Vilafranca, to purchase as much garlic as he could find, since that town, together with Banyoles, was the Liliaceae's main market.

They drove through a large piney wood on the way to Ordal. The air was perfumed. The dark green trees clustered on the hillsides. Occasionally they would glimpse a bare rock or a landslide that had occurred who knows how long ago, probably in ancient times, occasioned by remote geological factors. A few minutes ago they had enjoyed the company, seen from various angles, of Montserrat's imposing bulk, described by Laborde, invoking Humboldt, as remarkable for *"la composition, la conformation, l'arrangement et la position des rochers dont elle est couverte. C'est un composé de pierres calcaires, de sable, et d'autres cailloux unis ensemble avec un mortier, et formant l'espèce d'agglomération connue des naturalistes sous le nom de pouding."*

They had passed the hamlet of Palma and the Xipreret and Lledoner Inns and were heading toward Ordal, still at a furious pace. Novau, who always felt happy in the open air, waved his handkerchief every time they passed a farmhouse or saw people on the road.

"Nature's wonderful!" he exclaimed. "Three cheers for nature!"

Their pace had now slackened. The road twisted and turned,

clinging to the sheer and stony mountainside. Rocks of granitic aspect loomed up, along with dangerously steep cliffs. The horses sweated beneath the sun, their sleek hides glistening. Montpalau rested his silver-headed walking stick on the carriage floor and contemplated the district's strange configuration. A jumble of disconnected thoughts went through his head, upon which the *Avutarda geminis* superimposed itself, unknown and undetermined, confused with a certain strange, deformed, and monstrous presence. He carefully avoided formulating its disagreeable name.

At last they reached the mountain's crest. Through the shimmery heat, they spied Barcelona in the distance. They stopped at the New Inn, where their horses drank while they dipped almond cookies in sweet wine. A few wagoners were there, all cursing uproariously.

The road became smoother and the landscape softened. In Vilafranca, Novau bought a large quantity of braided garlic that they loaded on top of the carriage. Something strange then occurred, utterly indefinable, a kind of dazzling, blinding tension, as the Liliaceae's sharp odor spread through the air. While his cousin was shopping, Antoni de Montpalau took a stroll through the walled town, which contained a military governor, a mayor, eight aldermen, a big parish church, three monasteries, and one convent. He visited the Virgin of Sorrows' Chapel, famed throughout the area. He counted twelve distilleries devoted to the production of brandy. Monsieur Laborde believed the town had been founded by General Hamilcar Barca, who had named it Cartago Vetus because it was the first Carthaginian colony on the peninsula.

They dined sumptuously at Beco's Inn and continued on their way. A great drowsiness stole over them as they slowly digested their meal, and they dozed off until late in the afternoon.

They drove through vast vineyards. The setting sun's oblique rays illumined the graceful leaves; the grapes turned golden in the soft evening light. They were small, polished beads, distilling all the earth's sweetness. Twisted vines laden with fruit stretched away to the horizon. From time to time, a cart would emerge from a lane or smoke would rise, vague, distant, and weightless. Peace floated in the air and gently enfolded the landscape. The road was protected by a double row of huge plane trees whose foliage was so thick that it formed a kind of long, vaulted tunnel. Occasionally, they passed an irrigation ditch full of pitch-black water on whose surface they saw a leaf or those waterbugs peasants call "weavers." Then the frogs would suddenly fall silent, and when the horses approached would swiftly leap into the water with unexpected little splashes.

As they rounded a bend, they caught sight of Arboç's rooftops and steeple. Night was falling. Antoni de Montpalau thought it imprudent to venture further and decided to end their first lap in that town.

They entered Arboç through the Barcelona Gate. At the inn, they were most favorably impressed by the cleanliness that the mistress, a pretty girl named Pepeta Freixes, had imposed. They chose their rooms and spoke for a while with Pepeta, who was friendly and hospitable. Pepeta saw to all their needs and served them a cordial, very stimulating after a day on the road. She said it was made from a secret recipe she'd inherited from her mother, may she rest in peace.

To pass the time and whet their appetites, the two young relatives went out to stretch their legs and stroll about. It was a very neat town, with all its houses brightly whitewashed. They were surprised to see such an abundance of women. The girls, all of them lovely, sat in the doorways. Wherever the two friends went, they could hear bobbins clicking. Everyone was weaving lace. The lace makers chatted with one another across the streets and smiled saucily at our two young and handsome gentlemen. A little embarrassed, they wandered among all those women, stealing shy glances at the prettiest hands and faces. They agreed that, though Monsieur Laborde had scarcely mentioned it, the town of Arboç should be known far and wide as one of Cata-

Ionia's most delightful and charming spots and, moreover, highly suitable for a relaxed vacation.

Unfortunately, our friends lacked time for such peaceful repose, since in truth, it was urgent that they quickly reach their destination. Lamenting this regrettable circumstance, they returned to the inn with those bobbins still gaily clicking in their ears.

Bandits

JUST before daybreak, Novau and Montpalau set out
again on their journey. Though the morning air was
cool, they had been warmed by some big mugs of steaming milk
and enormous slices of buttered toast.

Far away, Lichnowsky, who was suffering from insomnia,
also rose. That morning he felt especially jumpy. He meticulously
folded his blanket and, leaning against an oak, lit a cigar while he
contemplated the rising sun. One of his men, who had stood
watch on a high moss-covered boulder, came and whispered
something in his ear. The prince picked up his saber and, followed
by his man, entered the woods, where they crouched down and
waited. A lark sang.

Everything was quiet. The horses, however, whinnied nervously. Amadeu did his best to control them. Montpalau opened a
window, leaned out, and asked if anything was amiss. They could
barely see, for the morning light had just begun to dispel the
darkness. All one could hear were the horses' whinnies and their
uneasy trot. Novau loaded the pistols.

They had crossed the Gornal, beneath the picturesque
Maidens' House, and were halfway to Bellveí. The landscape was
so deserted that it seemed uninhabited. They began to make out
the outlines of things, which came forth slowly and uncertainly,
as from an underground burrow. Suddenly a cry rang out, followed by some shots that flashed from a grove of stunted trees.

Amadeu whipped the steeds, which broke into a gallop.
There was no doubt that someone was after them, for soon they

spied ten or twelve riders in hot pursuit. Then day broke, and they could clearly see a disorderly band of armed men. Since they wore no uniforms, one thing was certain: They were not government troops and at best might be Carlists, though their appearance suggested ordinary brigands. Antoni de Montpalau and his cousin hesitated not an instant. They started firing alternately through the two windows, producing a certain dismay among the attackers, who had not anticipated such a resolute response.

Man is forged in battle and in love. The battle must be just; the love must be pure. Otherwise virility will founder on the rocks of abjection and remorse. Meditating on these exalted and noble themes, Prince Lichnowsky watched clouds scurry across well-known skies above landscapes dear to his heart. But in fact, they were absurdly distant and unreal. The prince felt a vague premonition that something was occurring somewhere, something his chivalrous soul reproved. Lichnowsky had been raised according to harsh military ideals in princely Graetz Castle.

The carriage tore along at a furious clip. Unexpectedly, a wagon piled high with hay appeared, blocking their path. Amadeu calmly maneuvered the horses off the road and set out across the fields. Montpalau, between shots, ordered him to drive onto a hill to their right. There they would defend themselves properly.

And indeed, once they had reached the indicated spot and were armed with those high-precision English rifles, they decided to follow Marshal Vauban's rules. Amadeu climbed onto the roof amid the garlic, Novau crept between the wheels, and our hero remained at the window. Once three lines of fire had been established, the attackers' situation became a trifle uncomfortable, since this tactic proved to be highly efficacious.

After a fruitless charge, beaten back by our friends' marksmanship, the unknown pursuers changed their tactics. They dismounted and took up positions all around the carriage, though at a prudent distance from it.

This was not at all to Antoni de Montpalau's liking, for he

calculated that they might spend ten days as easily as ten minutes trapped there—a thought that had little appeal, given the circumstances. Ideally, faced with such well-organized resistance, their foes would have beat a retreat—an orderly one if you will— and abandoned their initial plan of attack. Anything else seemed to place our friends in grave jeopardy.

As Montpalau had foreseen, six hours later the situation remained unchanged. That is, it had worsened. Amadeu shouted that he was running out of ammunition. Novau cursed, lamenting his awkward position between the wheels, which caused him cramps and other, more trivial inconveniences. Montpalau wondered whether a desperate sally would not be best. Anything rather than be trapped like rats.

Just when Fortune seemed to forsake our friends, a bugle sounded. Almost simultaneously, a volley startled the besiegers of that improvised fortress. Behind them, a battalion of the queen's infantry advanced in formation, commanded by a valiant brigadier. The besiegers found themselves in a tight spot, and though at first they prepared to resist, they soon abandoned the effort, for the officer, showing his skill and courage in a calm but devastating maneuver, was about to cut off their only means of escape. In view of this development, the unknown attackers mounted their steeds, which they had left behind a barrier of calcareous nature, and fled in shameful disarray.

Montpalau and his friends stood up, cheered the victorious troops, and ran to embrace the valiant captain who had saved their lives. From a nearby ridge, a solitary horseman contemplated the scene.

A sigh of relief, like a butterfly, like a disintegrating wisp, took flight. The prince mounted his steed. Once again, he felt sure of himself. A pine branch trembled imperceptibly, while a squirrel, with nervous movements, gnawed a cone. A strong smell of wet earth rose.

Our friends were taken to the walled town of Vendrell, where they slept at the National Militia's headquarters. Everyone treated them with great solicitude, and the mayor delivered a passionately liberal speech. Antoni de Montpalau said he had no idea whether their mysterious attackers were affiliated with any group. He felt there was a certain resemblance, however, to that unexpected assault in Gràcia.

Speaking with the brigadier who had rescued them, Montpalau asked if he thought the assailants were Carlists.

"Never!" he replied. "I fight the Carlists not only out of conviction but by profession. An attack on civilians is, according to the Eliot Convention, an act of brigandage. Don't forget, however, that there are bandits who disguise themselves as Carlists."

They went on conversing for a while. The day's emotions, however, had been exhausting, and since on the morrow they had to continue their journey, Montpalau decided to retire to bed.

He said goodbye to the valiant brigadier, who was setting off that evening to relieve the siege of Ripoll. Suddenly, Montpalau resolved to write to Baron de Meer, describing the officer's brave conduct and urging his promotion.

"Your name?" inquired Montpalau. "I ask, of course, in order to remember it forever in undying gratitude."

"Joan Prim i Prats," the brigadier replied, snapping to attention and saluting.

That night, Montpalau and his friends nostalgically recalled the wonderful cordial made by Pepeta Freixes in Arboç.

On the Path to Adventure

THE sun shone brilliantly. *The Young Observer,* however, published this somber note:

"Catalans: The infamous usurpers, aware of their impotence and impending destruction, vile and cowardly by nature, instead of begging our beloved sovereign for mercy have stooped to absurd intrigues in order to sow uncertainty among us.

"This royal junta has brought to light the bizarre machinations of a certain self-styled naturalist, well known for his nefarious liberal views, who, for unknown but dubious scientific reasons, seeks to infiltrate our ranks in the company of another personage and a servant. This publication, which proudly deems itself your leading organ, filled with admiration for your heroic virtues and unsullied loyalty, will confound such wicked schemes, proving that your breasts harbor but two sentiments: love of God and love of king. The junta, therefore, will take all necessary precautions. Catalans: its members, proud to be sons of this country, where laurel bushes sprout everywhere, watered by your ardent blood, determined to triumph or perish in your company, certain that you will justify their sentiments, will keep you informed of any further treachery. Our noble Catalan spirit scorns such lowly intentions—Royal Junta of Berga."

To compensate for Antoni de Montpalau's wicked plots— since as the astute reader will have surmised, this article referred to him—*The Young Observer* then printed an impassioned sonnet:

Salve, salve, O beloved monarch!
Long live King Charles, victorious and great!
Thy valiant minions, with righteous hate
Have spilled their pure blood, to thy banner rallying.

The perfidious traitor brazenly tried
To rise up against thee, haughty and proud;
But on this day, with martial clamor loud
We have bested our foes with ardor and pride.

Engrave in marble and bronze the story:
Unforgettable deeds of combat and war
That will soon determine the fate of our Spain

And donning the laurels of victory's glory
Hasten to Madrid, O worthy conqueror
Preceded by the love of a people free again.

Unaware of the Junta of Berga's diatribe against himself and his companions, Antoni de Montpalau, having recovered from the previous day's mishaps, now strolled with Novau through the streets of Tarragona. They wished to visit the famous cathedral —though only briefly, since their battle had already cost them a day and they were eager to move on. Moreover, as they had passed through Altafulla, Montpalau had spent a few minutes honoring the memory of Martí Ardenya, one of the town's most illustrious sons and an outstanding scientist.

Monsieur Alexandre de Laborde must have been little impressed by the beauties of Tarragona, since his respected guidebook only mentioned the city's negative aspects: narrow streets; filth; a total absence of broad avenues; bad inns; ugly, crumbling houses, etc. He even considered the cathedral crass, characterless, and quite laughable compared to those in France.

His views were not shared by our young naturalist, who

stared in wonder at the cathedral's filigreed beauties and unique adornments. They strolled through the vast nave and marveled at Saint Thecla's grandiose alabaster altarpiece. Montpalau also registered, with an expert eye, the splendid tomb of that archbishop whom Pere Gil had mentioned: Don Antoni Agustí, the papal legate. As they were leaving the cloister, they heard a strange noise: Whoosh! Whoosh! Turning around, they beheld an enormous owl perched on a cornice beneath the dome, staring at them blankly.

Deeply moved by the grandeur of their nation's history, they left the cathedral. Montpalau copied from a memorial tablet an inscription that he planned to send to Bartomeu Garriga:

> C. AEMILIO. C.F.
>
> GAL. ANTONIANO
>
> AEDIL. II. VIRO
>
> FLAMINI
>
> AEMILIAE. C.F.
>
> OPTATAE. AN. XVI

The sun brought out the stones' honey color. Pilate's House stood majestically by the sea. The marble and cypresses, as always, lent classical scale and measure. Montpalau thought of Catalonia's eighteenth-century thinkers.

They left imperial Tarraco and set out on the road to Reus. Alexandre de Laborde, whose itinerary headed south toward Valencia, took his leave of our gentlemen. Soon he would reach Cambrils and l'Hospitalet de l'Infant, whose inns he would revile with great gusto.

With its delightful smell of roasted hazelnuts, Reus pleased them even before they reached it. They passed Saint Peter's Church and observed the grain merchants' stalls. Montpalau had a close friend in Reus: Josep Veciana i Sardà, member of the Academy of Science, some sixty years old, a widower with two daughters. He owned a beautiful house furnished in exquisite taste. He invited our two gentlemen to lunch.

When it was time for dessert—that is, at one o'clock on the dot—Veciana's daughters sang two duets—"Il bacio furtivo" and "La lacrima grossa"—in pathetic tones and with sweetly modulated voices. Ursula, the elder, was engaged to a captain of the chasseurs stationed in Reus. Carmeta, her younger sister, was still unbetrothed.

The two gentlemen praised the damsels' beauty and good manners and congratulated Veciana on being so favored by Providence. After chatting awhile, they asked about the best route to Pratdip.

"Pratdip, I've been told, is amply endowed with *Aconitum lycoctonum*, commonly known as wolfsbane," Veciana replied. "The shortest route is through Montroig, but I wouldn't recommend it, since that scoundrel Llarg de Copons operates in the area."

"My God!" Montpalau exclaimed. "Then which way should we go?"

"Via Falset. Given the conditions around here, you should move from one military post to another. Otherwise you'll be risking your lives. It'll take you a bit out of your way, but you'll be safer."

Montpalau accepted Veciana's prudent suggestion. He still felt shaken by their last scrape.

They stayed a while longer with the academy's distinguished member. He was a genuinely charming man. Finally they set out for Falset.

Falset is the capital of the Priorat. Surrounded by rugged mountains, it was a stronghold of the first order. Fortified and manned by a battle-hardened garrison, it was considered safe from Carlist guerrillas.

Dusk was already falling on Falset the impregnable, on its noisy forges, on its noble edifices and taverns thronged with wine and brandy drinkers, when our friends entered its narrow, ill-lit lanes. As required, they called upon the head of the garrison, presented their safe-conduct, and were about to rest their weary bones in the first inn they found when a messenger from the Baroness d'Urpí appeared.

The baroness, informed by her brother of Montpalau's departure and his plan to investigate the strange events in Pratdip, had sent her overseer to await him in Falset. She assumed they would pass that way since, as Veciana had pointed out, it was the safest route.

The overseer was a tall, gaunt, taciturn gentleman dressed in black. He explained that, if they set out that night, they could reach Pratdip by daybreak. The baroness urgently needed them and would wait up until they arrived.

Resigned, Montpalau acquiesced. He thought it would be indelicate to deny the wishes of an anxious and imperiled baroness.

Pratdip

PRATDIP is a village in an area dominated by high, craggy mountains covered with aromatic pine groves and swift, icy streams. Huge granite boulders contrast with occasional strips of red and fertile soil tilled by industrious peasants. The area's greatest riches, however, are its sturdy goats, which, dauntless and persistent, seek out their own food.

A curious naturalist from Tortosa, Sir Cristòfor Despuig, listed Pratdip's graces in 1557: "First of all, you will find the world's loveliest springs, cold and clear, and in particular one should mention Ashy Spring of fearsome strangeness, for every Friday or Saturday its waters turn ashy as though they had been poured from a pot of cinders, while on other days they are clear and sparkling. One can also find most plants needed by apothecaries, along with fragrant mountain flowers in infinite abundance and wild fruits and nuts, including chestnuts.

"These mountains are endowed with a marvelous variety of trees: common pine; aleppo pine; oak; kermes oak; maple; pomegranate—these last two especially good for making chairs—fir; yew; beech; elder; buckthorn; honeysuckle; juniper; hawthorn; hazelnut; holly, from which birdlime is made; ash; juniper; and savin. The mountains offer us countless gifts, especially wild mushrooms in such abundance and of so many types that one can scarcely believe one's eyes. A great many of these are good to eat, while others are inedible but useful for other purposes, and there are also truffles, along with superb jet, quicksilver, and iron ore.

"You may well believe that these mountains harbor far more wildlife than the plains, such as boars, deer, mountain goats, martens, genets, badgers, lynx, squirrels, rabbits, hares, wolves, and foxes, along with such birds of prey as eagles, falcons, goshawks, and sparrow hawks, nor do the streams lack trout, eels, barbels, or bream. There are also gold and silver mines, and in one area called Gimp's Hollow one can find rubies, emeralds, and garnets."

Pratdip, then, surrounded by this veritable orgy of wild mushrooms, goats, partridges, lettuce, and emeralds, stands upon a mountaintop crowned by a ruined castle. Beneath it lie broad meadows, which surely account for its name, and the surrounding countryside is about as green as can be: pale green, apple green, ashy green, bright green, purslane green, pensive green, eerie green, Dip green, etc. There's a big communal irrigation tank filled with green water and, at the entrance to the village, a majestic fountain with several spouts offers the visitor a melodious marvel—cool, green, and refreshing.

The village is tiny, and as you leave the highway, the first thing you notice, apart from the castle, is a large house made of fine cut stone. This is the modern residence, as it were, of the Barons d'Urpí and has been ever since the castle was abandoned in the sixteenth century. The traveler approaching Pratdip is serenaded by a choir of clucking chickens. And a cloud of feathers floats in the air.

Antoni de Montpalau's carriage wended its way through deep, misty valleys and along winding mountain roads toward its final destination. Beside Amadeu sat the Baroness d'Urpí's overseer, silent and hieratic, his arms folded. Inside, the two gentlemen dozed uneasily, often waking with a start.

Before they left Falset, Novau had peeled an entire braid of garlic and, after assuring himself of the cloves' potency, had strung them around the carriage for protection. Whether for this reason or by chance, a dozen large bats fluttered nervously about, keeping out of range of the garlic, uttering shrill satanic cries and stubbornly escorting our friends till the early morning, when they finally sighted Pratdip.

They drove through the walled and despairing town. Groups of women in mourning prayed aloud in the streets. In the windows, one saw bouquets of wilted purslane. A procession with lit candles slowly wound past the church. Black crape fluttered on door knockers. Death ruled that mass of living corpses, that land soaked in tears.

They stopped outside a large, stone doorway. The gloomy overseer leapt down and led them up a broad staircase flanked by polished wooden banisters. A handful of servant girls came out to welcome them with sad smiles. At last they entered a spacious room where, exhausted, they collapsed on a sofa.

Novau couldn't stop yawning. Soon a door opened and the baroness appeared, followed by her daughter.

The two gentlemen kissed the baroness's hand. She was a lady of aristocratic features, some fifty years old, most courteous. She spoke with great vigor. Her daughter was extraordinarily beautiful, dark skinned and vivacious, and her air of energetic authority suggested that she was her mother's second-in-command.

"Dear gentlemen," said the baroness, "I would like to introduce my daughter, Agnès. I am both pleased and grateful that you have shown such interest in this regrettable state of affairs. Please excuse my impatience to see you, but I was anxious to consult such a notable man of science. Later we shall speak of these matters. Now you must rest. My daughter will show you to your rooms."

The two cousins bowed to their hostess.

Agnès led them to the quarters that had been prepared. They walked down long, wide corridors flanked by old hope chests, climbed some stairs, and left Novau in his comfortable chamber. They continued down the hallway, turned right, and descended three steps. Bright sunlight streamed through the window. A child's voice drifted in:

"Damsel Agnès
Would you fain be robbed?
Yes, if the gallant
Makes my heart throb."

Montpalau pretended he hadn't heard. Agnès looked at him intently. Her gaze was keen and caressing, soft but steady. Montpalau felt slightly awkward.

The *Aurea picuda* barely commenced its ineffable song. It sang in a register inaudible to human ears. Nonetheless, the reminiscence of a shadow, impalpable and attenuated, caught the silent melody and shuddered. Finally, it disintegrated in the morning's cool, woodsy scent.

"Sleep well," Agnès said. After closing the door, our naturalist stood pensively for a few minutes.

The Tactical-Scientific Defense

THE Marquis de la Gralla felt most impatient. He eagerly awaited news from Pratdip, from his sister and Montpalau. He weighed various hypotheses about that bizarre occurrence, feeling a morbid preference for the most fantastic ones. One might say it was a private preference, since in public he was constrained to defend rational explanations in accord with his position as a scientist and his learned colleagues' views. Occasionally he had called them together to discuss risky theories about nonexperimental physics, but, as is customary in such cases, the discussions had turned into veritable battles in which Bartomeu Garriga's irascible character and Segimon Ferrer's perpetual ill humor were amply displayed. The Marquis de la Gralla's little group was like a ticking bomb whose fuse had been lit amid sulfurous fumes by Pratdip's unknown vampire. This bomb, if not neutralized, would burst into a multitude of deadly mathematical-botanical, theological-physical, and medical-musical fragments, destroying the harmonious equilibrium maintained for so many years by the marquis's aristocratic authority and Antoni de Montpalau's tactful moderation.

Such was the situation in Barcelona. In Pratdip, our hero threw himself into his activities. After resting all morning and eating lunch, he summoned the town's leading lights in the baroness's name and explained, with profuse details, the scientifically unproven possibility that a vampire was at work. He noted the strange anomaly represented by the presence (albeit only in legend) of such a being in Catalonia, since vampires (and one had to conclude that a vampire and the Dip were one and the same, given their identical activities) had seemed to pertain exclusively to the Balkans. In fact, this was the first known case not only in Catalonia but in all of Spain. He declared that, although science had found no plausible explanation for vampires' disconcerting existence—for the simple reason that no scientist had ever seen one—now he, Antoni de Montpalau, the Academy of Science's most modest member, was prepared, if the Dip really existed, to seize the unique opportunity it offered to trap, study, and destroy it using the scientific method, or, should the opposite be the case, to proclaim its nonexistence to the four winds as a figment of the popular imagination and to explain its deadly effects in a rational fashion, tying them to some empirical cause that naturally escaped him at the moment. He went on to say that reason obliged them, in the present circumstances, to accept, a priori, the Dip's hypothetical reality and take appropriate precautions. To protect themselves from that singular being's activities, they must consult the works of experts in demonology, fortifying their spirits in the belief that such a state of affairs must soon cease. To ensure such an outcome, he had forged a plan that, for the moment, he preferred to keep secret, and until the time came to put it into practice, they should employ garlic, pectoral crosses, parsley, and mirrors in addition to purslane, which he saw was already widely used in Pratdip. These measures would serve to hold the vampire temporarily at bay. He and his cousin and assistant Isidre de Novau would later show the townsfolk exactly how to use these antidotes. He concluded his talk by exhorting those present to trust in the efficacy of science and to spread the principles of tactical-scientific defense among the inhabitants of Pratdip.

He was warmly congratulated. Montpalau drank a glass of water that Agnès brought him after his speech and, contemplating his listeners' faces, he had the impression that he had managed to raise their morale.

The mayor, who bore the curious name Magí Peuderrata,

asked Montpalau if he thought it opportune to post a ban giving instructions.

"An excellent idea," replied Montpalau. "Draw up a ban summarizing what I have said and announcing that tomorrow before sundown I shall inspect all the houses to ensure that they are properly protected. At the same time, I shall distribute whatever antidotes the villagers lack."

Having spoken, Montpalau inhaled a little snuff from his tiny, handsome box. At that moment, in some indeterminate place outside the baroness's house, an inexplicable contortion occurred, a sheaf of wrathfully compressed air that sent out impalpable ripples, like incipient sighs or lamentations, snuffed out before they began to take shape. A diffuse tremolo fluttered in an ideal sphere with no concrete existence, propagating itself and, as always, swiftly disappearing.

Later that afternoon, our celebrated naturalist shut himself in his room to pore over thick volumes and papers yellow with age. He found some interesting observations about the subject of his research in a monograph entitled *Memorandum on Pholades or Mitylus lithofagus* (sea worms), which cast light on secret relations and the nature of latent life. Above all, however, he was intrigued by a paper whose author, the distinguished Basque naturalist Juan Manuel de Ferrery, had been a member of the Philosophical Academy and the French Scientific Institute. This sage had led an exciting life, and his name was closely linked to that of Saint Faustina. A great traveler, he had been very active politically. In recognition of his many investigations and discoveries, Pope Leo XII had granted him Saint Faustina's body, intact and uncorrupted. With the Holy Father's blessing, he transferred her remains from the Roman catacombs to his native village, Pasajes de San Juan. After an undetermined period in which he respectfully experimented with the holy relic, Ferrery, seeing that he was old and would shortly undertake that voyage from which no man returns, donated Saint Faustina to his parish church. For this reason, he is still revered as its greatest benefactor and his name is associated, as we have mentioned, with the saint's. Juan Manuel de Ferrery died in the year 1818 in Bayonne, France, and was laid to rest in the church at Pasajes de San Juan, only a few feet from the tomb in which the venerable damsel Saint Faustina's remains lie, still intact.

It must have been about six o'clock when a steward interrupted our young and illustrious botanist's ruminations, announcing that the baroness, who had a visitor—a learned Dominican friar—wished to introduce them and, if it was not too much trouble, she hoped he would join them in the drawing room.

Montpalau didn't wait to be asked twice. He found the baroness and charming Agnès seated on the sofa, conversing with a monk of gentle and intelligent aspect. A Valencian named Jaime Villanueva, he was on his way to the monastery of Scala Dei, where he planned to copy some documents referring to that glorious edifice. He said he was publishing, volume by volume, an ecclesiastical history of the Catalan-speaking areas that would expand, in a certain sense, the work of the eminent Father Florez. The friar was clearly a remarkable man.

Villanueva and Montpalau felt an immediate and intense mutual attraction. Montpalau told the historian, who already knew about the baroness's difficulties, why he had come to Pratdip.

His interest piqued by Montpalau's explanation, the ecclesiastical scholar offered to collaborate, within his own field, in resolving the enigma. Their methods were different but might complement each other. Perhaps some explanation would come to light, hidden among the archives' dusty documents.

"Precisely," replied Montpalau. "As you put it so aptly, our methods are different. Scholarship operates through accumulation; science through synthesis. We must, therefore, seek their point of convergence."

The conversation lasted a while longer. Agnès kept her eyes fixed upon Montpalau. Her steady gaze disconcerted him. He stumbled over his words—he, who was usually so sure of himself.

Antoni de Montpalau tried to focus on the Dip, on that un-fathomable mystery. He wasn't sure he could manage it.

Evening fell. Pincers gripped their anxious hearts. In its daily defeat, the sun surrendered to the realm of darkness. Villanueva recited Saint Ambrose's hymn:

"Aeterne rerum conditor,
noctem diemque qui regis
et temporum das tempora
ut elleves fastidium,

praeco dici jam sonat
noctis profundas pervigil,
nocturna lux viantibus,
a nocte noctem segregans.

Hoc excitatus Lucifer
salvit polum caligine,
hoc omnis errorum chorus
viam nacendi deserit."

Hope was focused on the star that gives us daylight. Aurelius Ambrosius's sepulchered voice, in noble competition with that of Saint Hilary of Poitiers, intoned the Church's loftiest hymn.

The *Phallus impudicus*

THAT night, the Dip claimed six souls. The towns-people were desperate. It was a high point in that invisible marauder's career. Peret Minosca, the cutler; Leopoldo Núñez, the bailiff; Pauleta Vinyes, the sandal-maker's wife; Josepet Aulés, the gravedigger; Llúcia Terradell, the midwife; and Enriqueta Moles, the tax collector's seven-year-old daughter, were all victims of the vampire's thirst for human blood.

Antoni de Montpalau examined the corpses. They seemed drained, dry as bones, as though someone had emptied them out. It was a grim spectacle. Montpalau winced at the families' despair, their sobs and anguished imprecations. Nonetheless, his scientific attention focused upon two fateful little holes of perfect round-ness in the neck of each corpse. There was no doubt. The vital fluid had been extracted by suction through those two perfora-tions. These had been produced by two sharpened canine teeth of a sort found in no known species of animal. The vampire, or whoever committed that abomination, had operated with me-ticulous precision. There was no time to lose.

Montpalau decided to inspect the area around Pratdip, since the village itself seemed to offer few clues. He ordered Amadeu to fetch his carriage, and at eight that morning, he rode forth with his faithful cousin Novau. Naturally, his first thought was to visit the cemetery. High weeds ran riot within its crumbling walls. Incised in stone, one could read names and professions. There were faded wreaths, old black ribbons, and all the iron crosses, without exception, had been eaten away by rust. Novau tried to open the gate to a moss-covered mausoleum and was surprised by a sinister creak. One by one, Montpalau scrutinized the tombs, all of which seemed perfectly sealed and intact. They found nothing out of the ordinary in a village graveyard. A lark sang, perched in a carob tree.

The air was clean, freshly washed. The trees were sharply outlined against the sky, as after a rain. A big locust hopped about near a patch of fennel. A woodpecker on a blackberry bush eyed it attentively.

They followed their noses. Amadeu set out down lanes they abandoned when more promising ones appeared. Occasionally, with lit torches, they entered dark caves. Montpalau scrutinized the most trivial anomalies: a fox's tracks, a fallen leaf, a slug's slimy trail. They strayed deep into the woods, far from the village. They felt they were seeing places no man had ever laid eyes upon. Amadeu, suddenly gripped by an intense colic, asked Montpalau's permission to retire for a moment.

The two relatives waited. Seated upon a fallen tree trunk, they smoked peacefully amid the sounds of innumerable birds.

"Sometimes I wonder if I'm dreaming," said Montpalau. "It's all so absurd, so utterly chimerical."

A few pine needles crackled. Novau spat upon a clump of thyme. Then he stared curiously into his cousin's eyes.

"There are things your mentality cannot fathom. Because there are clearly things that are beyond science. In the end you'll be forced to admit it."

Suddenly they heard screams and saw something crashing through the woods. Amadeu emerged, his face contorted with horror. He was stumbling, and his brow was beaded with sweat. He managed to stammer that, seeking a suitable spot in which to satisfy his needs, he had come across a monument erected by the Devil. He couldn't describe it. It was something monstrous—and indecent too.

The two gentlemen decided to see what this was all about. They calmly followed Amadeu, and when they had gone about two hundred paces their eyes widened in amazement at the sight of an enormous mushroom, more than two yards high, shaped exactly and shamelessly like a male genital.

"A *Phallus impudicus!*" Montpalau exclaimed in wonder. "And what an extraordinary specimen! In the last century, Francesc Castelló i de Malla found one two feet high near Vic. One this large, however, is totally unheard of."

Amadeu calmed down. Montpalau took off his frock coat and, in shirtsleeves, measured that terrifying mushroom's height and diameter. He felt feverish, inspired. He, Amadeu, and Novau began to dig away at the dirt around its base with flint rocks, which abounded in the area. He urged them to exercise extreme caution and delicacy lest they damage the remarkable specimen. He had decided to uproot the mushroom and send it to the Academy of Science in Barcelona. There they could replant it or petrify it through a hydrolytic process of his own invention.

Suddenly it occurred to him that he couldn't show up at the baroness's house with that compromising piece of sculpture. This thought worried him so much that he broke into a sweat.

He quickly began to search for a solution. They had to find a way to hide the mushroom's brazen shape. Their frock coats weren't big enough to cover that gigantic affront to morality. Finally, he decided to send Amadeu to fetch two double sheets from the baroness's house on whatever pretext he could think of.

Meanwhile, they continued to dig. When Amadeu returned an hour later, Montpalau had achieved his goal. Despite its size, the mushroom weighed very little, since its basic element was cellulose. They gently wrapped it and, having cushioned it with armfuls of soft young grass, tied it to the carriage roof.

Returning to Pratdip shortly before lunchtime, they hastened to the carpenter's shop and ordered a wooden crate seventy-eight inches long and eighteen inches wide, to be ready by late afternoon. They'd pay whatever it cost. They left the *Phallus im-*

pudicus's veiled form at the carpenter's shop, warning him neither to approach nor touch it lest he suffer a grave misfortune. These words made a deep impression upon the honest workman.

Lunch at the baroness's house was sad and silent. The Dip's six victims seemed to hover about them. Montpalau caught an imploring look from Agnès.

Late that afternoon, having written a report to the Academy of Science, Montpalau showed up at the carpenter's house with Novau and Amadeu. They carefully placed the *Phallus impudicus* in a magnificent crate with reinforced corners. The mushroom looked like a mummy wrapped in a shroud. As soon as the crate was nailed shut, they bore it to the carrier's office, where they instructed him to ship the shameless fungus to the academy's representative in Reus—Josep Veciana i Sardà—who in turn would see that it reached Barcelona.

Evening was drawing on. As they went out into the street, they spied the mayor, Magí Peuderrata. Together they formed a committee to inspect the houses and ensure that they were well protected. First, however, they went to collect the antidotes stored at the Urpí residence.

Montpalau told the mayor that the most effective preventive measure was the stench of raw garlic, which would hold any vampire at bay. Purslane and parsley were less potent. Pectoral crosses kept off the vampire's attacks but not his presence. As far as the mirrors were concerned, they served to identify him, for no mirror would reflect a vampire's image. If anyone could pass in front of a mirror without being reflected, that person was a vampire.

Astonished by these revelations, the mayor summoned the mailman and night watchman. The two municipal employees set to work peeling garlic and soon had filled a bucket. Following Montpalau's instructions, they then fashioned wire hooks and speared a clove on each one.

With these ingredients in hand, the committee went through the village house by house. Montpalau entered every room, counting the windows and other openings. Then the committee members hung a clove of garlic in each one. Afterward, Montpalau distributed as many crosses as there were people in each house. As they left, he hung mirrors outside the doorways, repeating his explanations and warnings.

They finished just as night fell. As they stepped into a street, a huge, diabolical cat crossed their path, glaring balefully at Montpalau. Our hero, however, had grown used to such apparitions and gave the matter no further thought.

When they reached the Urpí residence, the committee disbanded. They all wished each other good luck and good night.

The Souls of Plants

THE Junta of Berga, in an urgent communiqué bearing the same date as the previously related incidents, informed Prince Lichnowsky that it had received a request from a Carlist guerrilla known by the name of "Owl," who acted, according to his own declarations, absolutely alone and at night in an unusual but most effective fashion in the deep woods around Pratdip. The above-mentioned guerrilla, wishing to normalize his situation by joining His Paternal Majesty's forces, asked the royal junta, while respecting his independence and particular mode of action, to appoint him colonel in the regular army, for such was the rank that he believed he had won through his victories to the greater glory of Charles V. Uncertain of the truth or falsehood of such affirmations but considering that, if true, it would be a great help to know that the traditionalist cause could rely on an ally in that area, and wishing, on the other hand, to avoid any false step that might cover it with opprobrium, the junta asked Prince Lichnowsky, as the commander closest to Pratdip, to conduct as thorough an investigation as he could of the aforesaid allegations, operating with his customary wisdom and discretion, prudence and speed.

A cock crowed. It was six in the morning. Prince Lichnowsky finished reading the communiqué and scratched his head. The special courier who had brought the missive sipped rum from a cup near the campfire. His uniform was dirty, and he had a six-day beard. He held his horse's reins in one hand. Suddenly a carob tree's branches, controlled by some peculiar contraption, hid the scene from view. Only the trembling leaves remained, along with a distant vision of Vimbodí's steeple.

At the same time Pratdip's townsfolk, swept along by a wave of delirious rejoicing, toasted Montpalau's victory, for his tactical-scientific defenses had worked and the Dip, for the first time, had been foiled. The baroness warmly congratulated Montpalau on his brilliant success, while Agnès gazed at him with intense and significant gratitude. Montpalau, as usual, felt something odd in the pit of his stomach.

Several days passed in this fashion. Every evening, the committee replaced the cloves of garlic, ensuring that no opening had been left unattended.

After a week, Montpalau convened the town's leading lights again in the baroness's name and, taking the floor, expressed himself in the following terms:

"As you have observed, the defenses I proposed have been effective. I congratulate both myself and all of you on the exactitude with which you interpreted my instructions. The Dip—or whoever he may be—has been reduced to impotence. But he continues to exist. The cause remains, my friends. Until now, all our measures have been preventive. Yet we cannot spend our lives hanging garlic cloves in windows and glancing into mirrors. We must enter a second phase and eliminate the cause. We must destroy the Dip."

At this point, the listeners' applause and frantic shouts of approval forced Montpalau to stop. Once they had calmed themselves, he continued, "Some days ago, I mentioned a plan of attack that I wished to keep secret. The time has now come to unveil and apply it. Because of his prolonged fast, the Dip must find himself in a state not entirely conducive to clear thinking. Enraged, I should say, against a well-protected village. Therefore, I suggest that, precisely now, when the vampire is blinded by his delirium, a window should be left open, unprotected by pestilential garlic and revealing a propitiatory victim within. He will surely appear. And be trapped! For hidden behind the vic-

tim, I and my assistants shall stand, holding all our most re-
doubtable means of defense. It will only last a moment—just
long enough to see his face. He will quickly be driven off. Then
the third phase will begin: his pursuit and destruction. This plan
is scientifically perfect, but it requires a victim—an apparent
victim, of course. I myself would like to be that victim, but as
you will understand, I cannot be both victim and pursuer, for I
require freedom of movement and an intense state of concentration. Therefore, I need a volunteer. A volunteer I promise will
come to no harm."

A sepulchral silence greeted our hero's last words. Long
faces and hostile looks swirled around Montpalau. Someone
whistled under his breath. The mayor, Magí Peuderrata, who
counted himself among Montpalau's assistants, roundly attacked
those present, accusing them all—females excepted—of womanly
cowardice and declaring them a most undistinguished group of
notables. All in vain. Panic, displacing the initial euphoria, seized
the audience, holding it in humiliating bondage. Neither taunts
nor sarcasm had the slightest effect. Montpalau felt deep dis-
appointment, a sadness arising from that spectacle of human
weakness. Then Agnès rose. Valiant, strong, determined, staring
into Montpalau's eyes, she said, "I shall be the victim. I formally
offer to submit, under your protection, to the Dip's malevolent
fury. I know I shall be safe in your hands, and that you will
protect my life as you would your own."

Simultaneous shock and relief greeted this sensational out-
burst. The baroness, pale as a sheet, desperately and obstinately
opposed Agnès's disinterested offer. Sacrifice her daughter, never!
Agnès remained unperturbed, her gaze fixed upon Montpalau,
the incarnation of dignity and nobility. The audience, after a
totally hypocritical show of resistance, praised Agnès's generosity
and accepted her offer. Amid the tumult, Agnès stood like a
rock in the wind, a heroic figure of exalted womanhood. The
baroness tearfully bowed to the inevitable. Speechless with admiration, Montpalau looked at Agnès. He could feel waves of

tenderness, deep and hidden resonances stirring within his breast. He had to control himself, to brake the impulse drawing him toward her romantic charm.

Hours later, in the old and majestic mansion's garden, Montpalau, having cut some fragrant red roses, offered them to her with these words: "I am proud of you, dear Agnès, of your firmness and resolve. I was moved by your faith in this humble servant of science—and of yourself from this moment on."

Montpalau was indeed moved. Agnès smiled, suddenly pale, small, and helpless. She bent over the bouquet our gentleman had offered her. Faint, enchanted music could be heard, like a delicate remembrance of the souls of plants.

The Vampire

PRATDIP'S castle was a smallish construction, part Romanesque and part Gothic. Hard to get to, perched at the top of the village, it looked out over a wide area. Abandoned since the sixteenth century, its towers and walls still conveyed a strange impression of force and power. Nature had invaded the castle, and bizarre weeds grew between its ancient stones; hawks and other birds of prey roosted among crumbling battlements. A vast melancholy emanated from those silent halls, abandoned to time's slow but inexorable devastation. On moonlit nights, the castle's aspect was still more fantastic.

Villanueva was greatly intrigued by the castle. He scarcely left the Urpís' library, where he sought information about the village's past and its ancient lords, the castle's masters. He felt certain that he would discover some explanation that fit in with our hero's scientific research. Using all his knowledge of paleography, he deciphered disturbing documents and constructed complicated family trees. Sometimes, he thought he spied a phosphorescent glow among those worm-eaten documents, and he set off eagerly on some diabolical trail.

Montpalau, meanwhile, had prepared a perfect trap for the vampire. No detail was neglected or left to chance. Agnès's bedroom was, so to speak, reduced; for Montpalau, needing space for himself and his assistants, divided it in two with some long curtains that hung from the ceiling. They placed the damsel's bed against these curtains, facing the balcony, while Montpalau and his assistants prepared to watch and wait. He split his men into two groups: He, Novau, and Amadeu would remain near

Agnès. Magí Peuderrata, the mailman, the night watchman, and four others who knew the countryside well would stand guard inside the mansion's front door, ready to sally forth in pursuit of the vampire.

The fateful hour struck. Agnès embraced her mother. Montpalau kissed the damsel's hand and assured her that he would be separated from her only by the curtain. If possible, she should sleep; in any case, she should pretend to sleep. The vampire on the balcony had to behold a sleeping body, breathing regularly.

At the last moment they hung a big gilt-framed mirror on the wall where it could be seen from behind the curtain. Everyone felt jumpy except Agnès and Montpalau, the two protagonists of the drama.

The clock struck twelve. Agnès slipped into bed. Montpalau, his cousin, and Amadeu sat down on some stools and modestly gazed through slits they had cut in the curtain. On their knees Novau and Amadeu held hermetically sealed pots of garlic cloves. Montpalau had proven to his satisfaction that, once they were opened, the stench from the garlic would suffice to drive off a dozen vampires.

The hours crept by. The moonlight's phantasmagoric glow reached the middle of the chamber. There was a dense, tormented, ill-omened silence. Agnès lay quietly, as though she were sound asleep. Montpalau and his companions sat still, scarcely breathing. Amadeu stifled a yawn, provoking an angry glance from Montpalau, who, as he had promised, was stationed right behind the headboard.

They could hear a termite gnawing at some piece of furniture. An instant later, without making the slightest sound, a shadow alighted on the balcony, partly blocking the moonlight. The shadow swayed like the wings of an enormous bat. Then they spied a tall man in a long cape. He stood there for a moment, immobile. Our friends' hands gripped the lids on their pots, their bodies ready to leap into action. Stiffly, the figure slid toward the bed. It passed the mirror, which, as expected, failed to reflect its image. Suddenly, moonlight illumined the vampire's cadaverous face—the same as on our hero's would-be murderer in the far-off town of Gràcia. A white face, stretched taut between two pointed, goatish ears.

The figure bent over Agnès's peacefully sleeping form. Then suddenly, our three ambushers leapt forth with uncovered pots. Agnès screamed hysterically. Montpalau held up a crucifix.

The vampire swiftly retreated. His face contorted with dreadful pain at the garlic's revolting stench; his entire body began to glow. Everything happened in a flash. The shadows deepened, welcoming the phosphorescent vampire, who tried to take flight from the balcony. The garlic, however, must have weakened him or damaged something in his organism, for, flapping his arms, he fell through the air and fled down the street.

Magí Peuderrata and his men immediately ran forth with lanterns and raced after the hated vampire. After securing the balcony with an appropriate antidote and followed by his assistants, Montpalau joined them and together they pursued the fiend, clearly distinguishable because of his phosphorescence. They crossed tilled fields, leapt over hedges, plunged into thick woods. It was a desperate race. The vampire traced a wide semicircle around the village, as though trapped within some imaginary boundary. Then he turned back again toward his point of departure. Dawn began to break, and, to their amazement, he suddenly headed for the castle, outlined against the light of the rising sun. Closely followed by his pursuers, the vampire entered its walls.

The pursuers burst into the castle. Montpalau, as though certain of the vampire's whereabouts, sought the steps leading down to the crypt. They found them near the highest tower, and the entire troop noisily descended. They entered the crypt, full of tombs and gigantic cobwebs. A herd of rats scurried into corners.

In the middle of the crypt, glowing feebly, they beheld an open tomb. They approached it, but all they found were the vampire's cape and shoes.

A sinister laugh, satanic and mocking, echoed through the crypt. Simultaneously, a beating of wings made them look up. A huge eagle had just taken flight through a broad window near the ceiling.

"Too late!" cried Montpalau. "But victory is ours! We've found the Dip's tomb; he will never return. Pratdip is free. First, though, we must break the spell."

Having spoken, Montpalau pulled a large, brilliant rock crystal heart from the pocket of his frock coat. Bending over the tomb, he placed it on the cape in the spot where the vampire's true heart would have rested. Then Amadeu and Novau poured in the pots' contents, and they sealed the tomb.

Pratdip's slavery had ended. The Liliaceae's scent floated in the air.

9

Love

PRATDIP rejoiced at its liberation in a procession honoring Saint Marina, that most efficacious virgin and the village's patroness:

> If God's divine grace
> Thou wouldst attain
> Copy blessed Marina,
> Gentle and humane.
>
> In the city of Antioch
> Our protectress was born,
> Sent by Jesus Christ
> To comfort the forlorn,
> To love God and Our Lady,
> Twin suns of her morn.

The virgin's shrine is eight miles from Pratdip. There are springs with icy water, hard and clear as crystal. Thick woods surround the shrine.

Antoni de Montpalau was declared Pratdip's savior, through Saint Marina's intercession. At Magí Peuderrata's urging, the town council voted unanimously to erect a monument in the main square to his perpetual memory. He declined this honor and instead suggested that they honor their virgin saint, of such aristocratic origins:

Her rich ancestors,
Of most noble stock,
Proudly took their stand
On the Church's holy rock,
Faithful members
Of God's obedient flock.

From her earliest youth
She despised and shunned vice
Deeming fasting and prayer
The paths to Paradise
And a nun's devotions
Salvation's blessed price.

The villagers intoned their hymns with steadfast faith and
tearful gratitude. The ceremony was solemn, and their chants
rose toward Marina, at whose feet lay an image of the deformed
and defeated Dip. The altar's base was adorned with glazed tiles
naively depicting local artisans at work, or—in dark green—
certain plants from the area: purslane, anise, millet . . . and in
the center, scenes from Saint Marina's life:

Outside the church door,
As in her life we read,
Suffering inclement weather
During five years of need,
Accused of murder by a daughter
Of Pandoquius's vicious breed.
When Jesus beheld
This humble damsel's ways
He asked her to dwell in Heaven
For the rest of her days
Amid the host that to Our Lord
Continually prays.
Great and glorious miracles

Love

This lady hath done,
The feverish through her graces
Recovery have won,
And for restoring eyesight
She is equaled by none.

Nor was there any better medicine for the Marquis de la
Gralla's uneasy circle than the extraordinary mushroom that
arrived one day. They all hastened to his house, where, amid
astonished exclamations, they measured the fungus, determined its
specific gravity, and, after an effort to transplant it in black earth
from the Pyrenees, decided that petrification would be the wisest
course. Montpalau's report was published in the academy's bulle-
tin, and extracts were reprinted, with appropriate sketches, in all
the leading European and American scientific journals. Father
Matons and Segimon Ferrer had a quarrel about the celebrated
mushroom's etymology—finally resolved by Bartomeu Garriga's
irascible erudition. The Marquis de la Gralla took charge of the
petrification, applying Montpalau's formula with unprecedented
success. Once the process had been completed, the mushroom
was placed in the academy's garden as a monument, beneath
which a marble plaque bore its discoverer's name, the date of
his find, and the name of its illustrious petrifier. These were
unique moments for the marquis, filling his usually calm and
contemplative life with excitement.

In Pratdip, people continued to sing their virgin's praises.
Sometimes the lumps in their throats made their chants a bit un-
harmonious. Kneeling, young and old sang as one:

Those lost at sea
Have at last reached salvation.
Fires have been quenched
Through her intervention
And from life's perils we are saved
By her adoration.

Those who humbly beg
For this lady's aid
With miraculous cures
For their ills are paid
And thus do her worshipers
Feel unafraid.

Upon reaching the shrine, they began to dance under the willow trees to bagpipe music. The celebration remained etched in everyone's memory forever. Agnès and Montpalau wandered through the woods, amid exquisite, swift-flowing streams, hearing music in the distance. A poetic halo encircled the couple. His heart pounding, Montpalau uttered the eagerly awaited words. No reply was needed. An ardent look from Agnès, and their lips met in a passionate kiss. Rapture filled those two noble and generous hearts. The souls of plants swooned in sympathy, and delicately entwined lianas formed the two lovers' initials. The *Aurea picuda*—his favorite, shy and gentle—intoned, in a joyous finale, a thrilling and unusually audible solo.

The baroness was especially pleased when, a few minutes later, the couple told her of their decision. Actually, she said she had rather expected it, for love cannot be hidden from the eyes of the experienced, and especially from a mother. She felt very happy. She congratulated herself on her connection with the family of a gentleman who, apart from his sterling qualities, belonged to one of Catalonia's noblest houses. She solemnly gave them her blessing.

That afternoon, they again paid homage to the virgin. Agnès and Montpalau squeezed each other's hands. Everyone sang:

Our patroness and protectress
Thou shalt always be,
Answering the prayers
We address unto thee,
Showering us with blessings
For all to see.

Love

If thou wouldst turn illness
Into joy and health,
Emulate Marina,
Our glory and wealth.

The afternoon slowly faded, freed forever from infernal presences.

A Carpathian Tale

F ATHER Villanueva's research revealed a great deal about the Dip's nature and origins. The baroness, Agnès, Isidre de Novau, and our hero were all seated in the old mansion's dining room when the illustrious historian recounted his fabulous tale.

Some caged goldfinches sang loudly in the courtyard. Everyone held his breath.

In the thirteenth century, during the reign of James I, King of Aragon and conqueror of Valencia and Majorca, Prat's castle had been ruled by Onofre de Dip. Onofre, while possessing a modest fortune of Mozarabic origin, distinguished himself in particular by the favor and respect he won through loyalty to his monarch and bravery in battle. When the widowed king celebrated his betrothal to Yolande of Hungary, he was naturally obliged to send ambassadors to that distant land, along with a retinue that, despite the Catalans' proverbial stinginess, was a sumptuous attempt to impress the nebulous court, of which no one had a very clear idea. One of these ambassadors was Onofre de Dip. The documents don't describe his mission, since the chancellery was very discreet about political-sentimental affairs. Nonetheless, we know that Onofre suffered one of the most dreadful experiences that can befall any mortal—a thousand times worse than death or Hell. Onofre de Dip, on his long journey toward the Hungarian court, was crossing the Carpathians, where on Saint George's Eve all the world's evil spirits gather, and spent a night in the beautiful Duchess Meczyr's castle. Peasants in the area—though Onofre of course was unaware of this fact—crossed themselves whenever the duchess's name was mentioned and kept as far away from her castle as they could. They said she was a *vrolak* or *vlkoslak*—that is, a vampire.

Onofre de Dip fell in love with the duchess. Or more precisely, the duchess seduced him. On Saint George's Eve, with reprehensibly lascivious but to some degree comprehensible intentions, he believed he had induced her to do his will. But when he bent over her ivory face, his ardent lust suddenly vanished in the revolting corpselike stench that issued from her mouth. It was too late, alas. Two sharp fangs pierced his neck, while children of the night howled outside. Onofre did not die; his fate was far worse. He turned into a vampire himself.

The documents then describe a most interesting series of liturgical exorcist exercises. In any case, Onofre disappeared from the King of Aragon's court. His inheritance was given to his nearest relatives—the Urpís—who, some generations later, abandoned the castle and moved to the mansion where they currently reside. Since then, however, Onofre, a living corpse, has returned periodically from Cracow to reassert his rights to his village, which from that date has been called Pratdip. When this occurs, the results are dreadful, as we have seen to our dismay.

Here the information becomes difficult to grasp, because the documents offer a series of cabalistic prophecies—in part already fulfilled. They say the vampire will be driven from Pratdip by a "new force," then they vaguely mention an owl. It seems that they also refer to a fratricidal war in Spain. The owl will serve a king; this "new force" will pursue and defeat him. The force will already be known to the owl, who will urge him, through premonitions, to desist from his task. At last, the vampire will find peace.

A long silence followed Father Villanueva's speech. Everyone felt amazed by his ghastly tale. Many previously impenetrable mysteries had now become clear.

Father Villanueva rose and took his leave of those present.

He had to continue his work on the volume about Scala Dei, and therefore he planned to set out for the monastery. Turning to Montpalau, he remarked that, as he had foreseen, their respective skills had complemented each other. He solemnly blessed the betrothed couple. Everyone kissed his hand. The sun was setting.

Hours later, furious galloping was heard in the street, followed by a great tumult downstairs in the entrance hall. It was the baroness's overseer, covered with dust, his clothes torn. When he could finally speak, he said, "The liberal forces were ambushed last night near Cardó. The attacker was a previously unknown guerrilla leader named the Owl. Afterward, he beheaded half the population of Tivissa. It makes your hair stand on end! I saw it as I was coming from Tortosa. He was shouting, 'Make way for the Owl! Make way for the Owl!' "

Montpalau silently and significantly looked at those present. Then, clasping Agnès's delicate hand in his own, he sadly said, "My work is not over, for I am bound to science, to humanity, and in a sense to the prophecy. Tomorrow I shall set out in search of the Owl."

PART
THREE

1

The Count of Morella

THAT most distinguished and excellent gentleman, Ramon Cabrera i Grinyó, commander of the Carlist armies of Aragon, Valencia, and Murcia and Count of Morella by decree of His Paternal Majesty Charles V, was a dashing figure. In lithographs illustrating the works of such contemporaries as Buenaventura de Córdoba or Antoni Pirala, he appeared in arrogant poses, nobly idealistic, in full military regalia. His face, whipped by all the winds of lower Aragon and the Maestrat, retained its lively and energetic aspect, and his words, inflamed by a heroically nomadic life, were grandiose and stirring when he addressed his troops or the inhabitants of conquered towns.

The Count of Morella had always enjoyed excellent health. He had taken part, on foot and horseback, in a thousand campaigns and had never complained of the slightest indisposition. For the last few days, however, he had been feeling slightly out of sorts. Not that any particular organ bothered him; it was more a lack of initiative, a strange volitionless lethargy. This sensation began at night and rose like the tide. In the morning he awoke feeling feeble and worn. His doctors Joan Martí and Carles Arissó, perplexed, attributed it to dyspepsia or simple ill humor, since things had not gone entirely smoothly for the Carlist cause of late. That morning Cabrera and his aides, Generals Forcadell and Llagostera, were poring over a map at their headquarters. Cabrera, who felt a trifle hazy, was sitting in a comfortable leather armchair.

"Gandesa, gentlemen!" he exclaimed. "Gandesa is the key to

three kingdoms. I shall never tire of repeating it. Whoever rules Gandesa rules Catalonia, Aragon, and Valencia. This map tells the whole story."

Forcadell, who was nearsighted, peered at the map. An extremely complicated orographic system nervously crisscrossed the paper. Amid the spurs of an escarpment, a black dot, minuscule and intense, indicated the liberal town, six times besieged.

"Your plan seems a bit risky," Forcadell ventured, "especially considering the inhabitants' intransigence and the proximity of General Noguera's army."

"I order you not to mention that savage wolf who slew my mother!" cried Cabrera. "I shall strangle him with my bare hands. He and his wretched rabble will end up in my power!"

Cabrera spoke with terrible grandeur. He had risen painfully to his feet and now trembled with rage and hatred. His two assistants kept their silence, not daring to contradict him.

Wearily, making a great effort of will, Cabrera regained his composure. He heard something like the beating of a bat's wings in his ears, as though they had sprouted on the back of his neck. He had grown too excited. From now on, he would have to try to control his temper.

They went back to the map. Lack of roads was the main obstacle. In such circumstances, it was useless to even think about artillery. At most, they might manage a couple of small-caliber guns dragged on logs. In any case, those cannon from the forges at Cantavieja were of little use. Last time one had exploded, killing both gunners. Their plan of attack was to surround Gandesa again and bombard it from Calvari as best they could. Cabrera, descending from Horta de Sant Joan like a whirlwind, would try to storm the town. Forcadell would command the army's two wings, while Llagostera, with three battalions of reinforcements, would guard the pass through which the Ebre flowed, keeping an eye on the road from Tortosa lest Noguera's troops surprise them.

On the military map, their plan looked feasible. No detail

had been neglected. They couldn't fail. Gandesa would fall to the Carlist forces.

Sunlight streamed through the window. They could hear swallows' cries outside, and looking down, they saw horses crossing the ashy fields with provisions for Morella. Cabrera liked to describe Morella as an eagle's aerie; and indeed, the famous general, safe in his imposing fortress, seemed like a bird of prey peering out into the distance.

Llagostera took a few steps toward a table cluttered with field glasses, jars, and other insignificant objects, and filled a pipe for his commander. He brushed a few specks of tobacco off his jacket and handed the pipe to Cabrera.

An orderly entered, wearing a Basque beret. He bore a communiqué from Solaní, who operated on the coast near Móra and Flix. The count read it, first with indifference but then with careful attention.

"This is rich!" Cabrera exclaimed. "If I felt in a better mood, I'd burst out laughing! It seems we've got a competitor. Solaní says an unknown Carlist general, who's called the Owl and operates only by night, has crossed the Ebre from Catalonia and, after entering our jurisdiction, has begun to exterminate entire villages. Solaní says the fields are red with blood."

The Count of Morella was about to utter one of his famous quips when he noticed that he was feeling a little woozy. He fell silent.

The wings of some fantastic nocturnal beast beat in his ears.

2

Gandesa, the World's Flower

I T had been raining for a few days, and the Ebre was full, swift, and majestic, overflowing with reddish water and perilous eddies. At one bend, a bizarre raft struggled to reach the other shore without being spotted from Miravet Castle, since no one knew if it was controlled by Carlists or liberals.

The raft bore a carriage, and a rudimentary sail fluttered on its mast. The crew consisted of three personages, two of whom manned the sail while the third manipulated a broad oar that served as their rudder. As the reader has surely guessed, they were our three friends in search of the Owl. Montpalau and Amadeu struggled with the sail, executing Novau's orders as best they could. Novau himself handled the rudder with great skill, for, as we know, he was an expert seaman. Thanks to their prudence and Novau's navigational skills, the raft reached its destination without excessive difficulties.

Montpalau immediately took their bearings with a compass. They had to find the road they had abandoned because the bridge was down. In their crossing, they had drifted south toward Tortosa.

There were big, thatched sheds for drying fruit and lush fields stretching away into the distance. The soil was very fertile. From the top of a hill, they spotted Móra, Benisset, and Miravet, as though set in a flowering garden. On the other side of the river were Cardó and Tivissa, ravaged by the Owl, and nestled among the rugged mountains beyond them, Pratdip.

Montpalau remembered bidding Agnès farewell. He saw her,

graceful and strong, sweet and fresh as a peach, standing in the doorway with glistening eyes. The baroness had given him an old silver rosary. Agnès, his beloved, had added a handkerchief she had embroidered especially and some perfumed locks of her hair. As they were about to set out, he had kissed her soft lips.

They found the road again. As they left Móra, they heard some frightened peasants talking about how, the night before, twelve liberal families had been drained of blood through some mysterious procedure in El Pinell del Brai, near Gandesa. Everyone assumed it had been the Owl. The peasants crossed themselves.

Upon hearing this, Montpalau ordered Amadeu to head for Gandesa, a town that, while not quite a military stronghold, was a bastion of liberalism.

When they reached the inn at Camposines, our friends had reluctantly to abandon their carriage, as from that point on the trails were fit only for horses. They left their tilbury at the inn, whose owner pocketed sixteen *rals* for storage and maintenance, and prepared to continue their pursuit of the vampire disguised as a guerrilla. First, however, they dined on a sensational roast with aioli, washed down with wine so strong it brought tears to their eyes. Amadeu took the liberty of remarking that, with the stench of garlic on their breath, they had nothing to fear from vampires. Montpalau, however, found this observation in bad taste and shot him a glance that quickly made him fall silent.

Mounted on three powerful and vigorous steeds, the travelers reached Corbera, which the popular muse had dubbed "the windowed." People said "Corbera the windowed" or "I'm off to Corbera the windowed." There was a charming song that went:

> Corbera the windowed,
> Gandesa, the world's flower.
> The slopes around Fontcalda
> Aren't getting any lower.

Fontcalda is a shrine a stone's throw from Gandesa, where homage is paid to the Virgin Mary. Just as Pratdip had Saint Marina, so Gandesa took pride in the Virgin of Fontcalda, worshiped in all the neighboring villages.

Our friends had scarcely left Corbera when, rounding a bend, they beheld Gandesa's steeple. After its sixth siege, the town's status was changed by the Spanish parliament, which declared it the LOYAL, HEROIC, AND IMMORTAL CITY OF GANDESA and exempted its inhabitants from taxes and military service for ten years.

Gandesa lived in a state of constant vigilance. Around it, the townsfolk had dug a trench six yards wide and four yards deep. The town had no walls, but all the entrances and exits had been barricaded and equipped with loopholes. In the steeple, a watchman from the National Militia kept an eye on the trails leading up to the town.

There was only one way left to enter Gandesa: through the Corbera gate. The head guard examined Montpalau's papers and, seeing that he was an important personage, immediately took him to the mayor, Josep Alcoverro. Alcoverro, commonly known as "Pep Kettledrums," occupied a grandiose, labyrinthine, baroque house directly across from the church's famous Romanesque colonnade. Montpalau told Alcoverro—who was a distinguished trial lawyer—why he had undertaken such a dangerous journey, and the man's jaw dropped when he learned what a threat the Owl posed to Gandesa. Naturally, Josep Alcoverro knew nothing about the efficacy of garlic as a defensive measure. He urged Montpalau to give a talk that evening at the Recreational Society, provided he was not too exhausted, so as both to inform and to alert the population.

Montpalau and his cousin were then welcomed with exquisite courtesy by Antoni Galvan, the village doctor, a well-read gourmet of rather Voltairean views. Also present were Oriol Mani and Josep Maria Pasqual, two jurists who wore dark glasses; Francesc Escoda, the postmaster, a great huntsman and singer of *jotas*; Josep Sol, a rich wholesaler and brilliant mathematician; and Pablo Ruiz, an apothecary and amateur philosopher, one hundred percent Aragonese, who knew the recipe for one of Spain's most delicate dishes: *espedo*. And finally, the notary Manuel Ocaña appeared: a liberal, Freemason, and rapturous polka dancer.

They took a stroll through the village, they warmed themselves with more strong wine, and they gazed at the starry sky.

After supper, Antoni de Montpalau mounted the podium facing the Recreational Society's auditorium, which also served as a dance hall. He was introduced by the mayor, who took the opportunity to pronounce some harsh judgments on Carlism. Then Montpalau, carefully weighing his words before his hushed listeners, explained his objective: to learn as much as he could about the Owl, that dreadful vampire disguised as a guerrilla.

As usual, Montpalau was received with enthusiastic applause and was warmly congratulated by Gandesa's notables. Before he left, the local glee club performed Rafael de Riego's liberal anthem.

The notables accompanied Montpalau to his inn, where a hard and creaky bed awaited him. Then, still marveling at our young scientist's wisdom, they returned to play cards at the Recreational Society.

A Bill

A T six-thirty the next morning, a terrific rumbling
woke our friends. It could only be the sound of a
bursting shell. Silence followed. Then another explosion, closer.
And still another. The walls shook and windows shattered, as
though a giant diplodocus were beneath the inn. One could also
hear the dry, repetitious sound of volleys. Someone cursed furiously in the next room. The rumble returned, along with the
shaking walls.

Montpalau dressed quickly. In the street, he saw Alcoverro,
armed to the teeth, running toward the barricades with a handful
of followers. All the authorities and notables he had met the day
before hastened past, each leading his band toward some previously assigned position. Montpalau had no trouble grasping that
the town was under attack by Carlists.

Still lacing up his breeches, Amadeu ran out of the inn.
Silent and intrepid, his top hat perched on his head, Isidre de
Novau smoked one of his strong cigars in the square and observed the shells' trajectories. He informed his cousin that, as far
as he could make out, the Carlists had tried to take the town by
surprise just before dawn and were now bombarding it from
Calvari.

The shells arched elliptically. When they landed, some of
them bounced high in the air, giving the inhabitants time to flee
their deadly effects. The Gandesians displayed remarkable courage. One heard cries of "Long live the constitution!" and "Liberty
or death!" Women brought ammunition and brandy to their

fathers and husbands, and many took part in the defense themselves.

Doctor Galvan hurried through the streets, ringing a copper bell. Behind him, a dozen men bore stretchers for the wounded. As soon as they saw a casualty, they lifted him onto a stretcher, covered him with a sheet, and continued their rounds. Galvan had stuck two big pistols through his belt. Whenever he passed a barricade, he made his medical corps halt while, swept away by exalted constitutionalist sentiments, he fired furiously at their perfidious attackers.

The noise was deafening. Prince Lichnowsky couldn't abide thunder, for nature unbridled filled him with dread. He was a lion in battle, but the sight of storms made his blood run cold. A classical spirit, he greatly admired his compatriot Goethe. This storm was tremendous; the smell of gunpowder filled the air. It was strange. Basically, Lichnowsky felt very disheartened, for he had accomplished neither of the missions entrusted to him. Unfortunately, he had lost track of that mysterious scientist's restless wanderings, and no one seemed to know anything definite about the Owl, their nocturnal guerrilla. The junta had told him, in this latter instance, to consider the case closed, since the best way to avoid ridicule was to deem the Owl nonexistent and therefore refuse him the rank of colonel.

A shell burst. Montpalau, Amadeu, and Novau continued their stroll through the streets and squares. Buildings often collapsed, covering the Barcelonans' impeccable garments with dust. Amadeu carefully brushed off their frock coats.

Over a wall hung a splendid and truly interesting *Solidago virga aurea* and a *Petasites fragans* whose evocative scent brought to mind that of a heliotrope. Montpalau plucked a blossom and voluptuously sniffed its fragrance.

Another shell burst, this one barely two steps from the strollers. They emerged on a steeply inclined street at whose end stood what Gandesians called "the Castle." In reality, it was a ruined building holding two cannon General Borso di Carminati had given them during previous sieges. These cannon were manned by two sensational gunners: Matias Sabater and Rafael Navarro. Both were court officers, and wherever their gaze alighted, so did their shells. Don Antoni de Magrinyà i de Sunyer, ex-president of the Deputation of Tarragona, recounts an incident in his history of the sieges of Gandesa in which the gunners' proverbial skill achieved an amazing result: One of their shells landed in the mouth of a Carlist cannon. Naturally, the two colliding shells produced a terrible and demoralizing explosion.

After chatting with the gunners and inquiring about their techniques, Montpalau cordially congratulated them on their skill.

Then our friends returned to their inn in search of those extremely up-to-date long-range English rifles. Montpalau decided they should station themselves in the church's steeple, from which they would have a clear view of the Carlist lines. It was an excellent idea. The panorama was splendid, and they saw a profusion of red berets, offering an exciting target. Nonetheless, Montpalau's tactic was to concentrate their fire on the enemy artillery. Their marksmanship was so perfect that the Carlists had to repeatedly replace their gunners till, weary of such slaughter, they decided to move their cannon. This was a great victory, since the Carlist guns had a shorter range than our friends' rifles, which had rendered their foes' artillery impotent.

At midday, the innkeeper dispatched a sprightly lad to take them lunch and to tell them that the inhabitants, deeply moved by their bravery, tearfully thanked them for their invaluable help.

To celebrate the artillery's neutralization and to infuriate Cabrera, who was watching the battle from a hill near Puigcavaller, the glee club roamed the streets, performing various selections. Rumor had it that Cabrera was ill.

In fact, the Count of Morella bravely led the battle from an armchair, occasionally feeling a strange sensation at the back of his neck, as though two membranous wings had sprouted there. His subordinates had organized the assault with nauseating incompetence. He decided to shoot a few of them.

A Bill

The Carlist troops achieved none of their goals. The Gandesians' courage was not so much courage as temerity. The two jurists bravely sallied forth and returned leading four pack horses loaded with feed. They were the toast of the town.

When the sun began to set, the mayor, Josep Alcoverro, a man who never minced words, stationed himself at the Corbera gate behind some wine casks. There he delivered a violent diatribe against reactionaries, prophesying a series of disasters that would befall their attackers.

Night fell, and with it silence. The shots gradually died away till everything was still. Militia volunteers, however, stood guard in the darkness.

With the dawn's uncertain light, they saw that the Carlists had abandoned their positions and returned to their mountain lairs.

This heroic action, along with so many others, caused the following bill to be introduced in parliament:

BILL

1. When the state of the treasury permits, the city of Gandesa shall be rebuilt in the name of the Nation and at its expense, bearing henceforth the title: IMMORTAL GANDESA.
2. In the city's main square, a column or pyramid shall be erected bearing the inscription: GANDESA REBUILT BY GRATEFUL SPAIN.
3. All militiamen and citizens who have defended their city shall be deemed mobilized for the war's duration and shall be paid for their services.

This bill may be found in the parliamentary records for 1840, second volume, first appendix to number 98, page 1289. Rubric: Congress of Deputies. The commission was headed by Catalonia's great friend, that distinguished gentleman Don Pascual Madoz.

4

The Land of Fleas

MONTPALAU and his assistants spent a few more days in Gandesa, basking in the populace's grateful affection. The apothecary and philosopher Pablo Ruiz organized an *espedo* outside town in a delightful spot called "the Springs." This dainty dish, invented by lower Aragon's transhumant shepherds, consisted of lamb tripe wound around oak branches and roasted over an open fire. Part of its excellence derived from the way it crunched between one's teeth, but its most exquisite and refined peculiarity was that it still contained the beast's excrement.

There were hogsheads of new wine and abundant cherry cakes, moist and sweet, of great evocative powers. Everyone felt in an expansive mood.

Doctor Galvan, who was an amateur poet, dedicated an ode to Montpalau's immortal deeds. The wine had gone to their heads. One of the poem's most lyrically effusive passages, inspired by a certain Latin author, read:

> In oblivion's stream
> My fame shall not die
> But rather soar with my praises on high.

A few days later, learning that the Owl had resumed his activities between Arnes and Vall-de-Roures, our two gentlemen, followed by Amadeu, set out on his bloody trail.

In Horta de Sant Joan, they visited the arcaded Gothic square and the Holy Savior Monastery, above which black ravens circled. The air was chilly, and they had to fasten the top buttons on their frock coats. The landscape had changed. It was wilder and more grandiose, with the Maestrat's peaks in the background.

They passed through Arnes, stopping to admire its town hall, and through Vall-de-Roures, where they visited the Gothic church and the castle. They found no trace of the Owl.

Nonetheless, a little old lady, knitting in a doorway, recited the following riddle:

"The Owl doth sleep.
To the mountain the snail doth creep.
Go by night to the forest deep."

She had them stumped. All their efforts to coax more information out of her were in vain. After pondering her words, they concluded that she meant the Owl was resting by day, as is customary with the undead, and that they would find him after dark in the mountains. It was perfectly logical.

They set out as hastily as they could for the Beseit Mountains. The landscape was breathtaking. As they climbed, the air grew crisper and cooler, while the scents of woodland plants and wild animals mixed in their nostrils. Soon clumps of *Asplenium trichomanes* appeared—commonly known as ferns and used to cure alopecia.

They passed beneath mighty and deafening waterfalls plunging into abysses; they found huge gurgling caverns like enchanted palaces; deep gorges yawned beneath kermes oak and scrub, and only their horses' sure instincts kept them from tumbling in. In the valleys' violet solitude, they sighted graceful deer, which Montpalau identified as rare examples of *Capra hispanica*.

Amadeu found a very strange spring. After a frugal meal, as Montpalau's lackey began to wash their silverware, he saw to his horror that the blade of the first knife had been eaten away by the water, leaving only the wooden handle. Montpalau forbade his companions to drink such high-proof water, which might affect the mineral substances in their bodies.

At this point, Amadeu began to feel uneasy. The Maestrat was a most bizarre and unsettling area. Montpalau, on the other hand, cheerfully collected herbs. The mountains suited Isidre de Novau, their brave and taciturn sea captain, to a T. He found himself finally cured of that disease caused by canned food.

They hadn't seen a soul in the Maestrat. Evening was approaching. They spied a half-ruined farmhouse. A man with feverish eyes came forth when they knocked at the door.

They decided to spend the night in that wretched farmhouse. They supped miserably. Montpalau advised them to sleep with crosses around their necks. They hung garlic cloves in the windows. They fell into a deep and refreshing sleep.

When the cocks crowed, they again set out on their quest. In vain they sought some village, some sign of the Owl. The odd man with feverish eyes had spoken very little.

Now they crossed a plain strewn with rocks. At first they were smallish, but they saw much larger ones ahead.

They started scratching themselves—first their thighs and then their entire bodies. There were thousands of fleas. They came out from among the rocks, attacking first the horses and then the men. Soon their skin looked raw and purulent.

Suddenly, among those distant boulders, they spied some black forms leaping high in the air.

"Giant fleas!" Novau exclaimed. "We're done for. One bite means certain death."

Montpalau anxiously glanced about, as though searching for something. Their situation was desperate. He hastily dismounted. He cut three pine branches with copious needles and, holding them like torches, lit the needles, from which thick and balsamic smoke began to billow.

Those monstrous fleas kept their distance. They were hideous, awful beasts. They greedily eyed the travelers. Awaiting their chance, they leapt about, reaching incredible heights.

Holding their fumigating torches aloft, the three riders made their way through that veritable host of giant fleas. Strangely enough, no flea tried to pursue them. When they crossed a stream of clear and limpid waters, the fleas remained on the other side, watching them closely but impassively. After a while, they returned to the region of cyclopean rocks, still leaping as was their wont.

Our three friends breathed a sigh of relief. They had clearly escaped a close brush with death.

5

The Capture

"ATOMS, which are tiny, imperceptible, and nearly invisible entities that can only be seen in rays of sunlight entering a room, bear the Plague's contagion from one body or place to another. For this reason they are called seminaries, as their malignant and pestiferous nature multiplies whatever is borne upon the air like an evil seed. Otherwise the contagion could not spread from one place to another, for air can neither decay nor change its nature and substance. And as the aforesaid air is incorruptible, whereas atoms, being mixed bodies, are subject to corruption, they rot and, using the air as their medium, enter us through respiration, infecting bodies and hearts with the ills they bear."

It kept on raining. The three Barcelonans were obliged to remain in Salsera, a dusty and decrepit hamlet they reached three hours after their adventure with the fleas. It rained cats and dogs, opening enormous craters in the ashy soil. These craters became ponds, breeding grounds for putrefaction and death. Swarms of larvae would emerge, pullulating at sunrise, in their nuptial flights and biological metamorphoses, infecting the very air they breathed. Montpalau amused himself by reading *Brief, Highly Useful and Profitable Regimen for Preventing and Curing the Plague. Written by Bernat Mas, Doctor of Arts and Medicine, Native of the City of Manresa. Dedicated to Our Lady of Good Health in the Year 1625. Under Royal License. In Barcelona by Esteve Liberós.*

The primary recommendations were: "First, ensure that the

surrounding air is pure, clean, and purged of all corruption, superfluity, and evil presences. Second, ensure that your body is clean and purged of all excess and ill humors. Third, your body should be fortified through preservative medicines and cordials against pestilent air. Fourth, flee any occasion that might rot or corrupt your bodily humors. And finally, resist sadness, melancholy, fear, and other passions of the soul.

"Bonfires should be lit around the city and in its streets and squares, using those things that most wonderfully purify the air, producing a bright, clear, and sweet-smelling blaze, like pine, laurel, olive wood, juniper, fir, ash, cypress, myrtle, savin, beech, orangewood, rosemary, thyme, lavender, sage, wormwood, southernwood, and other similar plants and trees.

"The city should be purged of rot, bad smells, and other indecent or discarded things such as dead beasts blocking the flow of sewers, pools of stagnant water, dung heaps, hides, soaking hemp, and tanneries if possible. The water in pools, irrigation tanks, ponds, and moats is most harmful; such recipients should be emptied and filled with earth lest foul odors infect the air. Dancing, merrymaking, and fencing tournaments should be forbidden, along with ball playing and other forms of bodily exercise, especially during the summer."

In the same spirit of scientific precaution, the Marquis de la Gralla and his colleagues crossed themselves in Barcelona after reading Montpalau's report on the vampire. The marquis felt that his theories had been vindicated and eagerly awaited further news about the mysterious being. Segimon Ferrer, the mathematician, maintained his skepticism, claiming that no conclusions could be drawn until Montpalau had examined the cause of those disasters. He had established the manner in which they took place, but it remained to be seen whether they were produced by some supernatural, legendary being. Personally, he doubted it. He was immediately rebutted by Father Matons, who, using rhetorical skills honed during ten years in the pulpit and through close readings of Gregori Mayans i Siscars and Antoni de Capmany, turned the conversation to questions of dogma and exorcism. Did his mathematical colleague mean to deny the Devil's existence?

Segimon Ferrer glared at Matons. Two opposing camps quickly formed. Bartomeu Garriga and Francesc Avinyó took Ferrer's side; the marquis and Samsó Corbella defended Matons. Josep Ignasi, the marquis's heir, followed the debate with the look of a man recently hit on the head with a club. That is, he had a most unworldly expression on his face.

Montpalau had often imagined the effect his report would have upon the marquis's circle. He smiled ruefully.

It had stopped raining. As Montpalau read and pondered, a Carlist cavalry patrol quietly surrounded Salsera. An officer with twenty men entered and forced our friends to surrender. Resistance would have been suicidal.

The officer treated them with great consideration. He was a gentleman. His name was Tomàs d'Orga, and he hailed from Xàtiva. He had fought in the Carlist armies since Baron de Hervás's time, when the rebellion had first flared up in the Kingdom of Valencia.

The patrol set out for Morella, Cabrera's craggy aerie. The sun slowly set. Wearily, a *Scaraboeus cervarius* ventured forth from its lair.

The Abominable Contamination

G ENERAL Ramon Cabrera was very ill. His doctors despaired; they had no idea what was the matter. Rumors circulated among the troops, who said some traitor was poisoning their commander. In effect, the command had passed to Forcadell and Llagostera, who sweated blood trying to fashion a viable plan of defense. Ever since Maroto's shameful surrender at Vergara, the situation in the Maestrat had been precarious. Between Espartero in Saragossa and O'Donnell in Valencia, Cabrera's aides lived in a state of constant apprehension. After their ill-fated attack on Gandesa, in which the general had still played a role, they had suffered a string of setbacks and reversals. Yes, life was grim in Carlist territory.

The Count of Morella, at that moment, sat pale and bloodless in his office, resting his head against a pillow. He suffered periodic and mysterious losses of blood. That much was clear. What his doctors could not fathom, however, was how he lost it. To counteract his anemia, they made him drink kid's blood and eat raw chopped meat. It did little good. He revived for a while, but on the morrow one could see that he had suffered another mysterious loss of blood, and he again heard—as is usual in cases of anemia—the sound of bat's wings in his ears. Lately, two small sores had appeared on his neck, which the doctors attributed to an incipient case of furunculosis.

He also complained of somnambulism. At any rate, he remembered absurd and confused scenes that took place during the night and were devoid of any logical meaning. Perhaps they were hallucinations caused by anemia and loss of blood. It was very strange. He recalled two fiery eyes, a jagged scar on a chin. One morning, as he was shaving, the weary general thought he saw his image become so translucent in the mirror that through it he could see the furniture behind him. He was gripped by terror.

Now Ramon Cabrera, with visible disgust, was eating some sheep's lungs, while Forcadell carefully went over their payments for cannon forged at Cantavieja, which were a source of constant worry to the general. Then they discussed Espartero's movements, closer and more threatening with every passing day. Forcadell didn't dare to mention their foe by name in front of Cabrera, and much less his recent title: Duke of Victory. Cabrera's fury would have shaken the castle's foundations. They also reviewed the hair-raising exploits of General Owl, who, as we know, had the insolence to operate not far from Morella, exterminating families of liberal views. Cabrera believed that the Owl—whom, however, no one had ever seen—hoped to profit from his illness, supplant him, and become the hero of the Maestrat. There seemed to be no other explanation. Cabrera trembled at this hypothesis, seething with indignation and eagerly awaiting the day when he would regain his good health and slowly strangle his rival with his bare hands.

He had just downed a glass of kid's blood. He wiped his lips on a coarse napkin, leaving a red stain. Forcadell asked if he would like his habitual pipe.

"No," replied Cabrera, emitting a staccato burp. Pointing to the door, he said, "Bring in the prisoners."

Antoni de Montpalau appeared, top hat in hand. He was followed by Isidre and Amadeu. Cabrera leafed through some papers.

Our hero immediately fixed his perspicacious gaze upon Cabrera's strikingly white face. He noticed the two small sores on his neck.

The Count of Morella, after reading Baron de Meer's safe-conduct, courteously addressed Montpalau: "I see that you are a distinguished man of science, but, at the same time, you are an enemy of our glorious King Charles V. The fact that we found you in our territory leads us to draw some ominous conclusions. Think carefully before you answer: What were you doing in Salsera?"

Montpalau remained silent for a few moments, attentively but discreetly examining Cabrera's furuncles. Then he gravely and laconically replied, "I'm searching for a vampire, one of the undead."

Cabrera started in his armchair. He felt those sheep's lungs turn to stone in his stomach. He asked, "What did you say? A vampire? I must be going deaf."

"No, general; I'm stalking a vampire. His name is Onofre de Dip, also known as the Owl in his macabre disguise as a guerrilla leader. This dreadful being is devastating the countryside, butchering parents and children alike and poisoning damsels' blood."

Staring intently at Cabrera, he added in a slightly lower voice, "The same being who, with diabolical persistence, has brought you to your present state. If God does not aid us, he will soon achieve his goal: to turn you into another vampire. Those two sores on your neck leave no doubt; they are his mark. Divine Providence, however, ignoring our ideological differences, has summoned me to your side."

An anguished scream greeted our hero's words. Clasping his neck as though he were choking, Cabrera sat bolt upright in his chair. He moved his lips, trying to speak. Then he slumped forward onto the desk.

Montpalau anxiously rushed toward him. Forcadell, who had followed the conversation with feelings that would be hard to describe, stood there in a state of shock. With Isidre's and Amadeu's help, Montpalau carried the Count of Morella to a couch and began to examine his inanimate body. Then, addressing Forcadell—who was on his knees reciting a paternoster—he ordered in a voice that brooked neither delay nor argument,

"Put two dozen garlic cloves in half a pot of water and let them simmer for twenty minutes. Then remove the cloves and bring me the water. One of my assistants will accompany you."

Forcadell left, still looking stunned and followed by Amadeu, who had become an expert in garlic-related matters. Montpalau, meanwhile, completed his painstaking examination of the general's body. Then he pullled a cross from his vest pocket and dangled it before the Carlist's face.

"No doubt about it," he said. "The blood is extracted by suction, as in the other cases. We'll have to act swiftly and decisively."

At that moment, Forcadell and Amadeu entered with a large, steaming caldron. They poured some of its contents into a cup. Six or seven Carlist officers peeked through the door, afraid to enter.

Montpalau, forcing Cabrera's lips apart, fed him a spoonful of the garlic water. He patiently repeated the procedure nearly a hundred times. When he finished, the sick man was certainly calmer. He had fallen into a deep sleep.

Then they bore the general to his chamber, undressed him, and put him to bed. There was a large window at one end of the room. The walls had been whitewashed, and their sole decoration was a framed letter from Charles V naming him Count of Morella. Beneath it hung two crossed sabers.

"We were lucky," our hero told Forcadell, who had finally regained the use of his voice. "We were nearly too late. I trust that, with a little luck, I shall be able to save your general."

"I thank you in the name of His Majesty and our entire army," replied Forcadell, visibly moved and clasping Montpalau's hand. "Thank you, gentlemen. I don't know how to express my gratitude."

"The general must never be left alone," Montpalau continued, "and especially at night. Trustworthy men must stand watch at all times. Every half hour, he should be fed three teaspoons of garlic water. This evening I and my assistants shall take all necessary precautions against another attack. Later we shall explain our techniques. Meanwhile, let the general rest."

At a sign from Montpalau, his cousin, valiant Captain Isidre de Novau who had once sighted the dreaded *pesce cola*, sat down at the bedside and lit his pipe.

Everyone else left. Montpalau softly closed the door behind him.

Outside, there was a kind of silent detonation. A gust of hot air wrathfully beat against the windowpanes. Nature's countless invisible tiny creatures froze for a moment. Something writhed in pain and desperation. A perverse shadowy form scaled a wooden fence, leapt over a stone wall, and fled through the fields.

Then a leaf, yellow and forlorn, fluttered down from a branch.

The Army Receives Its Orders

MORELLA is a striking city. Seen from the road that links it with Montroig—called Monroyo in Aragonese—it looks like something from the times of King Arthur and his knights, a most appropriate setting for the Holy Grail. The unsuspecting traveler, rounding the last bend in the highway, seems to behold a kind of landlocked Mont Saint-Michel, rising from the ocher soil complete with watchtowers, Gothic spires, and a lofty castle. Only the sea is missing. The sea, with its ghost ships and Breton crosses.

Morella is encircled by walls whose gates open onto the surrounding fields. Defended by huge towers, marvels of medieval military architecture, they lead into the city's tortuous streets. One immediately spies crumbling palaces, now silent, and illustrious ruins now used only by children at play. Morella's backbone is the long Carrer Major, a street flanked by arcades that keep off the sun in summer and the snow in winter. Halfway to the castle, one beholds Saint Francis's Convent and an extraordinary cathedral, both dating from the era of Catalonia's greatness. The cathedral is a jewel, profusely carved and with an ingeniously fashioned choir raised above the nave. Choleric priests with deep voices keep watch over its frozen glory.

The castle is perched on top of a mountain. In reality, the entire mountain is a castle, since military fortifications gird it in a spiraling pattern. Protected by powerful artillery, this fortress was deemed impregnable. It was Cabrera's headquarters. On windy days, one could see Charles V's banner fluttering on the highest tower.

Our beloved Barcelonans felt as free in Morella as three fish in the water. They were treated with great consideration and accorded all the honors reserved for science, but their legal status was a bit fuzzy since, as they were prisoners and foes of Carlism, there were theoretical limits upon their movements. In fact, however, they did as they pleased and won the hearts of both officers and common soldiers.

Montpalau, through his energetic protective measures, achieved positive results. Cabrera's room was carefully sealed with braids of garlic, and the water prescribed by Montpalau—together with copious and delicious food—revived the Carlist commander who, with the good cheer that always accompanies returning health, frequently invited our naturalist to share his table. The count's cooks joyously set about their task, preparing capons, hares, partridges, and roast suckling pigs.

Cabrera, as was natural, showed his affection and eternal gratitude to Montpalau, whose side he never left. Every day after lunch, they would take a stroll together.

Nonetheless, Montpalau was worried, for those two sores had not healed. There was something in Cabrera's face that was not to his liking. He gave him a string of wild garlic to wear around his neck. Montpalau's concern could be read in his gaze.

One afternoon, as they were drinking coffee on one of the castle's terraces overlooking the city, Montpalau said, "I'm going to tell you something that will require great fortitude on your part. Were it merely a question of your health, I would not say it; but it is also a matter that affects your very soul. Courage, general. The vampire's inoculative process, as you know, has been halted. All the same, anyone infected by the undead is himself a potential vampire. Should you have the misfortune to die before we destroy the Owl, your death would only be apparent, for you would then join the ranks of the undead. Only if we neutralize the Owl in your lifetime will you be freed from his curse. Your soul's salvation depends upon it."

Cabrera listened calmly to these words. His manly courage and resolve could be seen in his face.

"I suspected as much, dear Montpalau," he replied. "In a sense, I even knew it. I can see what the Owl wants and how few scruples he has. As soon as I realized that these sores would not disappear, I understood the full horror of my predicament. He wants to replace me, God help me! I trust, however, in His infinite mercy and your skill. In you the Owl has found an implacable foe, for though his powers are dreadful, you possess potent weapons: intelligence, valor, and learning. Moreover, you no longer fight alone. For the sake of humanity and to free myself from his curse, I place all my military, political, and economic means at your disposal. If the Owl wants war, let him have it. I shall rely on God and yourself."

That same afternoon, Morella's junta, both to raise the citizens' morale and to avoid malicious rumors, published the following ban:

> God Almighty, who decides all wars and who especially cherishes this faithful army and province, has restored the Count of Morella to health, curing the illness that for so long was the sole object of our concern.
>
> Immortal Cabrera, our century's greatest hero, has recovered. These comforting words echo sweetly in the souls of those he commands, from high-ranking officers to the humblest soldiers. All were weighed down by grief as long as our commander's life was imperiled. Clerics, men of the sword, civilians, rich and poor, aristocrats, plebeians—all felt the terror that afflicts a son who dreads his father's death.
>
> Now our weeping has ended, and we fear no longer. Let us turn sorrow into good cheer and, thanking Almighty God for our beloved general's recovery when he

appeared to have one foot in the grave, let us rejoice and celebrate his return to good health.

Your junta, unsurpassed in love for our most excellent lord, the Count of Morella, and in conjunction with the ecclesiastical authorities, invites those who dwell in towns paternally ruled by His Majesty King Charles V (may God preserve him) to attend a solemn Mass of thanksgiving. The service will be followed by two days of feasting, of whose exact nature we shall say nothing, for we trust that you will make this celebration far more glorious than anything we could devise.

Sons of the revolution, hideous monsters out of Hell whose deeds defile Spain, liberals of all stripes: You treacherously slay your best generals, while those who fight for God and our king's sacred cause weep, tremble, and ceaselessly pray for our commander's life. Herein you may behold your party's infamy and our honor and justice. Long live the Church, our absolute monarch, and the Count of Morella.—Jaume Mur—Manuel Garzon— Josep Maria Villalonga—Josep Bru—Lluc Domènec— Vicenç Herrero—Joan Baptista Pellicer—Francesc Bonfin —P.A.D.L.R.J.—Marià de Godoy, secretary.

Cabrera then dictated the following order: "Wanted dead or alive: a self-appointed general who goes by the name of Owl. This common criminal, pretending to represent our noble cause, has committed the most heinous and atrocious murders. His Paternal Majesty's government cannot tolerate the disrepute his deeds have brought upon us, as we know the aforesaid Owl is an agent of Freemasonry whom the illegitimate government in Madrid has sent to infiltrate our ranks in order to discredit us in the eyes of foreign powers.

"Consequently, I, Ramon Cabrera i Grinyó, Count of Morella and commander of the army of Aragon, Valencia, and Murcia, representing His Majesty Charles V, order all my troops to search for the Owl's present or former hiding places, paying special attention to cemeteries, crypts in abandoned churches, ruined castles, deep caves, and other places the common folk shun. Likewise, they should be forewarned that they will probably not find the Owl in person. All information on this particular should be transmitted to our headquarters. Morella. Count of Morella." The seal read: "Urgent."

8

The Cavern

PRINCE Lichnowsky decided that prolonged residence in Vimbodí had dulled his investigative skills and that it was time for a change. Since his spiderlike strategy had brought him no success, he would now adopt—metaphorically speaking—an opposite tack and imitate a locust's busy flight. He must find those spies who, under the pretext of a scientific expedition, were trying to infiltrate the absolutist camp. How? By going to Morella. Now he could see it all clearly. Their objective was the headquarters of Ramon Cabrera, Carlism's victorious eagle. He had been a fool not to see it sooner. He would set out immediately, disguised as a melon vendor. All he needed was a cart and some merchandise. Everything would go smoothly. Prince Lichnowsky smiled to himself.

Just as Prince Lichnowsky made this momentous decision, the invincible Ramon Cabrera, commander of the army of Aragon, Valencia, and Murcia, resolved—perhaps influenced by some telepathic signal—to abandon the city of Morella, leaving barely enough soldiers to defend it, and move his headquarters to Xerta. It was a bitter pill to swallow. Black clouds menaced the Carlist cause. Cantavieja and its excellent forges had fallen— alas!—to Espartero, the queen's fatuous general. O'Donnell was advancing up the coast. Count Charles of Spain had been assassinated under mysterious circumstances. Was the vampire a double agent? Had Providence forsaken their triumphant leader Charles V?

Cabrera and his army set out at daybreak. It was bitterly

cold, and all the officers wore mufflers. They had to get out of the Maestrat, to reach the Ebre's warm banks as fast as they could. The long column carefully skirted the area inhabited by the fleas, though one could see their prodigious leaps in the distance.

The guides decided that the best spot to camp was Enchanted Valley, where they would find plentiful stores of firewood. Streams of icy water flowed from unscalable peaks through groves of fragrant fir trees.

Antoni de Montpalau decided to explore a cavern whose terrifying mouth had caused it to be named Dead Man's Cave. The name seemed very suggestive; and it might easily be that the Owl, carried away by his peculiar inclinations, had chosen it as his daytime residence. It was a solitary spot. The cavern opened in the middle of a sloping plain. The troops pitched their tents around it so they could help if they were needed.

As usual, Amadeu and Novau accompanied Montpalau. At the last moment, valiant Forcadell also joined them.

After studying the cavern's black mouth for a few minutes, Montpalau pulled down his top hat, made indispensable by the humidity, and, with a stout rope around his waist, cautiously descended with a miner's lantern. His friends followed him.

The descent was slow and laborious. Finally they reached a kind of tunnel that, after a steep incline, led them to a chamber full of stalactites. The silence was awesome.

Having crossed this chamber, they entered another one, far bigger and straight out of *The Arabian Nights*. In the glow from their lantern, it looked like a casket lined with silk and glittering with rich colors: pale pink, emerald green, mother-of-pearl, coral-line red . . . At that moment, they began to hear extremely delicate music.

It was a kind of melodious, seductive breathing, frozen in time. They didn't quite understand what was occurring, but they felt a great desire to sink to the ground. It was like a distant choir of female voices, lost in the memory of things long forgotten.

Suddenly, they were gripped by terror and the certainty that something strange was behind them. They whirled around. A giant spider stood ten feet away, as though it had been turned to stone. That spider had no eyes.

They cautiously backed into another passageway whose walls were as transparent as glass. It led to a third chamber through which a black and silent stream flowed. There they were met by another surprise, very interesting to Montpalau from a professional standpoint: A huge white worm, also eyeless, stupidly curled and uncurled in a corner.

On the other side of the stream they saw two more passageways, one beside the other. They leapt across where the waters were narrowest and decided to enter one. The next chamber they reached was smaller and more intimate than the other. The scene that greeted them made their jaws drop with amazement.

Human figures turned to stone, frozen in varying postures, filled the cavern. Some were sitting or standing, while others lay on the ground as though asleep. There were mothers with children, as well as a dog furiously scratching for a flea. Montpalau concluded that some geological cataclysm had surprised that group of cave dwellers thousands of years ago, and he saw with satisfaction that nature's results closely resembled those he himself obtained through petrification.

Since no passageway led out of that chamber, they returned to the stream and, after discussing what they had seen, they entered the other passageway. Montpalau's heart was pounding.

The passageway led to a small chamber whose walls were black marble. On the right they spotted an old empty coffin that showed signs of recent occupancy. Nearby, on a raw pine table, they saw a sheaf of documents, an inkwell, and a pen. A pair of abandoned blunderbusses leaned against the wall.

As always, the vampire had eluded them. By the light from

the lantern, Montpalau read the papers. There were deeds to various estates and farms around Pratdip in the name of Onofre de Dip, along with some documents in Hungarian, incomprehensible to Montpalau, and Carlist propaganda from the Junta of Berga. He spied an envelope addressed in Gothic script, along with the beginning of a letter announcing someone's arrival and lamenting the fact that the writer had not yet been appointed colonel. It said that in any case his deeds had now earned him the rank of general. These protestations, however, had been rudely interrupted.

Everything conveyed an impression of disorder and precipitous flight. Montpalau turned to his companions and said, "I'm convinced that the vampire feels trapped. These papers indicate that, in a last desperate attempt, he's heading for Berga, but step by step, the prophecy is being fulfilled. Victory will be ours in the end, gentlemen!"

Once Montpalau had collected all the vampire's papers, they carefully retraced their steps.

As they passed through the chamber with the enchanted music, they saw the spider in the same position. Perhaps it had budged an inch.

Montpalau explained that the horrible monster was suffering the effects of petrification. They had to get away quickly because the petrifying agent was precisely that enchanted music.

No sooner had these words been spoken than they heard sweet mineral arpeggios.

9

What Is Written

A FTER a skirmish with O'Donnell's troops at Sénia,
where Cabrera had the bad luck to fall from his
horse, they reached Xerta before dawn. The Count of Morella
again saw his native region, the Ebre's rich and irrigated lands,
those farmhouses with a few palm trees clustered beside them.
They advanced slowly, stirring up clouds of dust; for apart from
the troops and cavalry, there were wagons loaded with supplies
and others bearing frightened Carlist families who preferred to
share their idol's fate.

A messenger arrived bearing bad news. Morella, after a few
days' resistance, had fallen to the forces commanded by Espartero, who saw his title, "Duke of Victory," embellished with the
words "and of Morella." Cabrera was so overcome by fury that,
had Montpalau not reminded him that his soul was in jeopardy,
he would have returned to make a last stand—a heroic gesture,
certainly, but one that sorted ill with his prevampire condition.
Cabrera had no business risking his life until Montpalau had
destroyed the Owl. What was more, they had to bend every
effort to capture him. They knew he was near Berga. No great
subtlety was required to understand what must be done.

Cabrera's sores began to bleed: a bad sign. He sweated with
terror and impotent rage. Montpalau had to double the dose of
antivampire tonic. The commander had grown horribly pale.

Another disastrous piece of news: General Zurbano had made
his way through the Beseit Mountains and was swiftly advancing

toward the Ebre. One could see a pincer movement taking shape, tightening the noose around the Carlist forces.

Beside himself, the commander of the armies of Aragon, Valencia, and Murcia called a meeting of his high-ranking officers and explained their predicament, while keeping quiet about his own personal troubles. They had to reach a decision, but which one? The officers remained silent. Their commander's attitude was sublimely heroic. Should they retreat toward Berga or stand their ground? The officers replied that Cabrera had their entire trust. They were ready to die for him. Therefore, he should decide; they would obey his orders.

The air was cool by the river. Big stone pools stood beneath vine-covered trellises. Sometimes the waters overflowed, and peasants used them to irrigate their fields. Children played by the river with wooden swords and paper hats. They also shot marbles and spun tops. They ran free along the banks and already knew the names of the different herbs in each village. Then they would grow up, become men, die and turn into hardy weeds growing amid the scrub, beneath the burning sun. If they raised their eyes, they beheld the firmament and everything dark and difficult, along with bright and shining things that no man could fathom.

The breeze was gentle and warm, rustling the flowering broom and bearing the scent of cherry trees. A wagon slowly passed in the evening light. A peasant burned some stubble.

Soon another messenger appeared, informing Cabrera that he had been named commander of Catalonia and head of the Junta of Berga.

What is written is written. Montpalau breathed a sigh of relief. The Count of Morella wept.

A mineral silence could be heard, a strange but agreeable metallic vibration. Suddenly, blending into the setting sun, a bolt of lightning could be seen across the river. The horses grew silent.

Turning to his officers, Cabrera cried, "Tomorrow we shall cross the Ebre to Catalonia. Long live the king!"

Montpalau helped the general to dismount. Night was swiftly falling.

PART
FOUR

Crossing the Ebre

Signora Matilde,

Io le avevo scritto un'altra volta. Le avevo scritto a lungo perchè il mio cuore nuotava nell'affetto e io non avevo un'anima in cui versarlo. Il mio pensiero era allora apresso in preda alla più terribile angoscia e io non sapevo che fare per alleggerirgliene il peso.

Ho sperato che Ella si muoverebbe a compassione se non di me, almeno du lui, Dio volle che l'affetto non corrispondesse al mio voto e Dio solo ne sa il perchè. Ma se io mi volgevo a Lei nel patimento perchè non potrò parlarle quando vivo nella fiducia e nel contento . . . Oh ch'io mi ricordi sempre del primo giorno che la vidi! ch'io mi ricordi sempre quel momento celeste in cui l'occhio mio affaticato si riposò sulla sua fronte.

Matilde, Matilde, oh! lascia ch'io t'ami sempre! deh! non distruggere questa illusione beata che si è incarnata in me! Lascia ch'io speri di vedere un giorno i nostri destini baciarsi insieme e confondersi in uno solo. Dimmi una sola parola di speranza, scrivimi una riga di conforto e l'anima mia si farà più leggera e l'amore più caldo.

—Felix Vicenzo

PRINCE Lichnowsky, after a last glance at the portrait in his medallion, addressed the envelope: Madame Matilde Leblanc—formerly Matilde de Ferrari—rue Saint Germain l'Auxerrois 15; Paris. He was writing by flickering candle-

135

light, filled with longing and despair, at an inn in Granadella. My God, when would this war be over? He had met Matilde on his last trip to Italy, at the house of Prince Colonna d'Este. His hopeless love dated from that visit—hopeless because the lady was married to a rich French wine merchant with interests in Burgundy.

Lichnowsky hitched his horse to its cart and decided to cross the Ebre at Riba-Roja, an unusual spot. He had followed a circuitous route, passing through villages whose existence was unnoted on any map. With special affection he recalled Pobla de Cérvoles, set in its lunar landscape, just the place to evoke his romantic love. *La mia vita, Matilde!*

At exactly the same time, our friends forded the Ebre in the opposite direction at Flix, a stone's throw from Riba-Roja. Novau again displayed his magnificent navigational skills, but only in aid of the civilians accompanying Cabrera; for, being a prisoner of war, he could not be forced to act against his convictions and the queen. The Eliot Convention was categorical on this point.

Cabrera ordered his cavalry across first, as the horses were unafraid of water and naturally good swimmers. Each rider bore an infantryman behind him. The operation was risky, but they had no other choice and had to act with dispatch and determination. Once they reached the other bank, those riders with sufficient strength returned and repeated the operation for love of the Cause. Many steeds faltered, and their riders drowned. The current swiftly bore their bodies downstream. Nonetheless, a not insignificant percentage of the army got across in this fashion.

The bulk of the troops were transported on three barges that the Count of Morella had filled with stones and sunk near Flix many years before. It had been a good hunch, given that at the time he had no idea whether they would come in handy again. The work went slowly, and Cabrera grew impatient. Six first-class swimmers took turns diving. Finally, when they had removed all the stones, they fastened ropes to the barges, hitched them to the horses, and dragged them onto the muddy bank.

Halfway through this operation, they were attacked by

O'Donnell's van, for most of his forces had reached Móra de l'Ebre. Llagostera, with the first battalion of chasseurs from Tortosa, took up defensive positions to protect the Carlist troops and, in a valiant and obstinate counterattack, drove the enemy toward the village of Ascó. Those rugged, ocher hills and dales were dotted with varicolored Isabelline uniforms and red Carlist berets.

Cabrera had to lie on a stretcher, from which he ordered his men about. Though exhausted, he felt hopeful that he would soon bring an end to that apocalyptic hurricane that had disrupted his life. Though he had never seen such a place, he dreamt of green meadows like those in Surrey, a peaceful bourgeois existence surrounded by setters, freed at last from the terrible undead.

"Courage, general," Montpalau said. "This is the beginning of the end. Fear not, for science is on your side. You still have your whole life ahead of you."

Cabrera smiled. He liked Montpalau. What a pity that he was a liberal.

Lichnowsky smiled too. Hidden behind some thyme bushes, he heard rifle shots and happily imagined a Carlist ambush of the queen's unwary troops. Beside him on a smooth rock, a small chameleon inched forward. From time to time it stuck out its incredibly long protractile tongue and caught an insect. It evolved with infinite caution.

Novau transported the Carlist families fleeing possible reprisals. There were gentlemen with noble faces who sadly contemplated, perhaps for the last time, their native land. Young mothers wept in resigned silence, with infants at their breasts. Amadeu helped Novau, manning the sail the intrepid captain had hoisted. The two men's humanitarian conduct won the Count of Morella's fervent praise.

"A truly heroic gesture," Cabrera mumbled, weakly and wearily. "We shall record it in gold letters, and you will be thanked by our king."

Now they ferried the supply wagons and their few pieces of

artillery across. It was hard getting everything onto the barges. One of the cannons forged at Cantavieja sank into the mud, and all their efforts to dislodge it were in vain. They abandoned it after carefully spiking it and pushing it even deeper into the slime. It was the only item of Carlist gear that fell into liberal hands.

Montpalau admired the courage and—why not say it?—the discipline of those much reviled troops. The military life shone with all its grandeur and self-sacrifice.

The last one to cross the Ebre's broad waters was Cabrera, protected by his trusty Tortosan chasseurs. Scattered gunfire could be heard. A dozen sea gulls from the delta soared above the river, alien and indifferent.

The afternoon grew milder. In the distance they could see Montsant covered by clouds. A soldier from Rasquera, gazing at the village, uttered the following words:

> "If Montsant wears a bonnet
> Rain's sure to fall upon it."

2

The Route

T H E Duke of Morella and Victory suffered an un-
pleasant surprise when he learned that Cabrera's
forces had entered Catalonia and were heading north. He had
counted on trapping them between O'Donnell's and Zurbano's
armies. Nonetheless, everyone was certain of the Carlists' impending defeat. Their Majesties, the queen mother and Isabella II,
had set out from Madrid on a triumphant trip to Barcelona, where
they planned to bathe in the sea, uniting medicine and politics.
Espartero, always astute and provident, published the following
ban:

> Bardomer Espartero, grandee, Duke of Victory and
> Morella, Count of Luchana, Her Majesty's chamberlain,
> Knight of the Order of the Golden Fleece, of the Dis-
> tinguished Order of Charles III and of Queen Isabella I's
> Order of the Americas, as well as of the military orders
> of Saint Ferdinand and Saint Hermenegild, holder of the
> Grand Ribbon of the Royal Legion of Honor, frequently
> decorated for his actions in battle, commander in chief
> of the national armies and colonel of honor in the
> princess's hussars, etc., etc.:
> When the pretender, bested at Urdax, was forced to
> seek refuge in France, those who served his unjust cause
> should have lain down their arms in acknowledgment of
> their errors. But accustomed as their generals were to
> profanation, theft, arson, and murder, neither the pacifi-

139

cation of the Basque provinces nor the amnesty I proclaimed upon my arrival in Aragon with the large army that accompanied me from the north of the peninsula induced them to desist from their criminal activities.

Only Catalonia still harbors enemies of our legitimate queen Isabella II and of those institutions recognized by the nation. But soon these foes shall be routed by the armies I command, and with pleasure I shall hear, in every corner of our kingdom, hymns of peace that shall supplant war's bloody cries. That this peace, the object of my unstinting efforts, may extend to Catalonia, undisturbed by rebels, murderers, and thieves who descend from their mountain lairs to spread fear and calamity among its villages, I deem it necessary to order, from this moment on and by means of this ban, the following:

1st article: Should any village council, upon sighting rebel troops or guerrillas, fail to notify our army's fortresses, columns, or divisions immediately, one of its members, chosen by lot, shall be executed and the rest sentenced to two years' imprisonment. Moreover, for each hundred inhabitants a fine of twenty thousand *rals* shall be levied to defray the costs of the present war.

2nd article: The authorities of any village in which one or more rebels are sheltered shall be held responsible, together with all inhabitants, under the terms of the preceding article. Moreover, the heads of all households in which they are hidden shall be subject to the death penalty.

3rd article: All rebels not in uniform shall be summarily shot.

4th article: All civilians bearing arms, separately or in bands, shall be liable to the punishment specified in the preceding article, as well as guerrillas and individuals who, separated from regular army forces, intercept mail, steal, or commit brigandage behind the lines of the armies I command.

5th article: All inhabitants not enrolled in the National Militia shall surrender their arms to our governors or commanders. Anyone failing to obey this order shall be shot, these being understood as the heads of households containing arms. Moreover, the offending village shall pay a fine of one thousand *rals* for every weapon seized.

6th article: Guerrillas surrendering to our governors or officers shall be given safe-conducts allowing them to settle in villages of their choice.

7th article: Any officer who fails to enforce this ban shall lose both rank and liberty. These orders shall be law from this day onward in regard to our foes, while all village authorities shall be held responsible for their implementation from the time they receive them, to which end the military authorities shall demand dated receipts.

Dictated at my headquarters in Manresa.

—Duke of Victory

These regulations had a depressing impact on Catalonia's Carlists, who, with the exception of a few fanatics, saw that their days were numbered. In Barcelona, the imminent arrival of Maria Cristina, known to favor the moderate party, provoked riots and demonstrations on the Rambles against the proposed Law of Municipalities.

Shots rang out. Speeches were made. The Marquis de la Gralla and Father Matons pored over treatises on telepathy and vampirism. The still-unclassified *Avutarda geminis* sat forgotten in its corner, glum and disconsolate, along with a letter from the "divine" Madoz y Fontaneda that lay unopened on Montpalau's desk.

Josep Ignasi, the marquis's heir, had recently invented the

"liberal flute," a pocket-sized instrument that, when blown, automatically played Riego's anthem. The instrument ensured that whole orchestras of flautists would attend all political demonstrations, both indoors and out. Josep Ignasi expected it to enjoy brisk sales.

Meanwhile, the Count of Morella's army crossed Catalonia, making straight for Berga and encountering no resistance. When they were five miles from Granadella, they veered toward Pobla de Cérvoles, skirting Montsant beneath a driving rain, and continued through the Llena Mountains to Albi, where they spent the night.

In these mysterious landscapes, scarcely known to a soul, Montpalau discovered a flying reptile—a survivor of the Quaternary Era—that possessed the rare virtue of also talking like a parrot. A Basque volunteer from Fuenterrabia, whose name was Arpiazu and who cooked for one of the battalions, took such a liking to the oratorical reptile that he offered to carry its cage and feed it. During their marches and countermarches it could be heard, amid pots and pans, singing an incomprehensible Basque ditty:

> Aztu, aztu gernikako
> Arrigola guetairá.

One day Amadeu, sick of its Carlist chatter, took it into the woods behind Arpiazu's back and taught it another ditty, this one brazenly liberal:

> To the constitution good luck,
> And a pox on that stupid fuck.

The couplet referred, of course, to the pretender Charles V, but Cabrera, who happened to hear it, thought it alluded to him and decreed, in a tumultuous fit of rage, that the bird would either be reeducated or forfeit its life. All their efforts to identify the culprit proved fruitless. Fortunately, the reptile went back to singing its Basque ditty.

On the morrow, the Carlist columns continued their march toward Vallbona de les Monges, where Montpalau had a rare opportunity to admire the tomb of Queen Yolande of Hungary in that celebrated and ruined convent, so rich in archeological wonders. The nuns, who led a strictly cloistered life, offered the Count of Morella and his officers sweet wine and cookies that they had baked themselves and that they passed through a little window. The poor sisters, whose economic situation was highly precarious, lamented their misfortunes at great length to Cabrera in the hope that he would plead their case before His August Majesty Charles V. After the Carlist officers had risen to their feet and sung a credo, Her Ladyship the abbess bade them God-speed and wished them every sort of success and prosperity.

Montpalau and his cousin, Isidre de Novau, politely remained aloof from these political exchanges so contrary to their convictions.

Having rested, the Carlist army continued its northward march at a quicker pace, crossing the Barcelona highroad at Hostalets, three hours east of Cervera. They pitched camp near Calaf, where they requisitioned a great number of chickens and rope-soled sandals. When the sun rose, with beating hearts and new footwear, the ghost army again set out for Berga.

3

Berga

A SHADOW stole across the rooftops, wound around a chimney that couldn't be seen from Santa Maria de Queralt, and took shape in the chilly morning air. It preferred garrets with sloping roofs, and the old cracked wood of dovecotes. Animals backed away, seeking some nook to cower in until it passed. Wearily, it unwound and, in a wisp of fog or smoke, flew almost invisibly to a better observation post. Then it began to wind around another corporeal protuberance, its muscles tired and defeated. The city huddled beneath it, gray and compact around the steeples on Saint John's and Saint Eulalia's Churches. Outside the fortified lines, beyond Metge's Brook, spread rippling fields, freedom, birds chased by brisk north winds.

Cautiously and slowly, the shadow slid down an old cracked facade. It halted at a window, gripping a half-closed shutter. Making a great effort, it slowly eased itself into the room and hung, scarcely visible, from the hem of a curtain.

The room was almost square. Its walls were whitewashed, and at the far end hung a portrait of the pretender. Six or seven men sat and waited, smoking cigarettes. They all had long faces and were dressed in black. Beneath the portrait stood a table with a tray of documents and a small bell. Behind it was an empty chair upholstered in red velvet. Everything had a musty and disordered air.

A guard wearing the Carlist insignia entered the room and announced, "His Reverence Father Torrebadella, president of this junta."

A robust and balding priest immediately appeared. Those present rose to their feet. Without a word, the priest strode over to the chair behind the table and sat down. Then, glowering at the opposite wall as though no one else were present, he said, "Gentlemen, Cabrera is at the gates of Berga. This is a matter we have discussed a thousand times. Had we sufficient forces, we would welcome him, as you know, with artillery. But Cabrera leads an army, and we have only Pep de l'Oli to defend us. Therefore, we must make the best of a bad situation."

"But General Segarra . . ." one of the councilors timidly interjected.

"General Segarra has told me not to count on his aid," the priest curtly replied. "He is busy in Campdevànol, preparing an action against Ripoll."

The priest drew forth a tiny box and calmly took a pinch of snuff.

"Count Charles of Spain's unfortunate demise," he continued, "let us admit it, has left us in an awkward position. But we only dismissed the count. In any case, responsibility rests with Segarra, to whose forces he was entrusted. We have nothing to hide, so let us show our faces. Segarra's strange behavior, however, will surely not pass unnoticed."

Hope lit up the faces of those present. With renewed cheer, they all praised the priest's astuteness. He rang the little bell.

"Order, gentlemen, order. We must proceed with tact and caution. We must be wise as serpents and gentle as lambs. Let us not be carried away by our impulses. First, we must assure that the Tiger of the Maestrat is in our pocket."

Everyone approved. Torrebadella pulled out a handkerchief of questionable cleanliness and, after a phenomenal sneeze that cleared his respiratory passages, added, "Relying on this junta's approval, I have given instructions that, as soon as Cabrera is spotted, a volley shall be fired from the fort at La Petita. That will be the signal. All the church bells will then ring. And we, assembled amid the populace's cries of joy (I should add that I have prepared the ground through my sermons), will throw open the gates to the invincible Count of Morella."

He paused. A bee beat against the window panes. There was also a wisp of smoke. He continued, "The general will be pleased by our humble welcome, our respectful deference, and above all by our serenity. He will also see (and this is important, gentlemen) that one of us is absent. A strange absence, to be sure, unjustified despite some vague preparations for a siege. He will ask, he will inquire. *Doubts will be sown in his mind.*"

Father Torrebadella laughed that grating laugh of his. At the same moment, a guard served the councilors some glasses of sugar water, a sad but healthful and soothing beverage.

A volley rang out. All those present, as though impelled by springs, leapt to their feet. The sinister priest, who had been stirring his sugar water with a spoon, greedily drank the last drops. He held out his hands.

"One moment, gentlemen. I must tell you that I have received another letter from that bizarre guerrilla named the Owl, offering his services and promising to rid us of Cabrera. His request has a curiously pathetic tone. All he asks for in return is a crypt in an abandoned church. As you will understand, we are dealing with a lunatic. I filed his letter but did not reply."

Everyone approved. They were feeling very impatient.

"And now, gentlemen," Torrebadella declared, "the hour has struck. Let us welcome the immortal Cabrera."

Having spoken, he made for the door through which he had entered. The members of the junta noisily followed him. Soon the room was empty.

Then something quite unexpected occurred. The fine wisps adhering to the curtain became a coil of black smoke, spinning dizzily and turning into a blurred human form. Incoherent words of blasphemous intent could be heard. The bee was superimposed upon and finally melted into the human head, and two terrifying, incandescent, satanic eyes glared forth. The swaying figure contracted, as though compressed by some inconsolable grief. Then it slowly dissolved till not a trace remained.

Meanwhile, the junta's members, led by their president, Father Torrebadella, formed two lines in the street amid the clamoring bells. Townspeople stood on the balconies.

They marched to the main square. There Pep de l'Oli awaited them with his ragged irregulars in red berets. The populace felt little love for them, as they were known to steal and commit all sorts of crimes.

Pep de l'Oli, a squat, red-faced, foul-mouthed gentleman, wore a dark purple beret. He raised his saber in salute when he saw the junta. He looked like a sans-culotte from the French Revolution.

From the roof of a building overflowing with excited spectators hung several fine damask bedspreads stitched together and adorned with big letters:

FROM BERGA

TO ITS GLORIOUS COMMANDER

RAMON CABRERA

LONG LIVE OUR ABSOLUTE MONARCH

The bedspreads' creases showed how long they had been neatly stored in linen closets. They were hung with elaborately and artistically tied ribbons. From the balconies, the populace saluted the junta's members.

The bailiff hurried up, bearing an embroidered cushion upon which a symbolic key to the city rested. He stationed himself on Torrebadella's left, two paces away.

At that very moment, a military band struck up a ponderous march. Clanging bells, martial music, screaming children, excited townsfolk, and bursting cannonades combined in enervating pandemonium.

They solemnly began to walk, as in a procession. The musicians led the way, followed by the entire junta and then Pep de l'Oli's battalion of undesirables. Last of all came the populace.

The gates were flung open.

Before them, in battle formation, terrible in its silence, Cabrera's army appeared. A group of officers came forth, led by the fearsome commander covered with medals.

Everyone's blood froze. Then Cabrera wordlessly led his men into Berga.

The Pathos of Horses

CABRERA'S first action as captain general of Catalonia, taken two days after he entered Berga, was to imprison the entire junta for the murder of his predecessor—that is, Count Charles of Spain. The case against them was painstakingly prepared, and the councilors, plunged into the black pit of despair, were locked in the basement beneath Saint Francis's Monastery, whose first floor was normally occupied by the royal armorers, some irascible Basque volunteers.

Cabrera reappointed the previous quartermaster general, Gaspar Díaz de Labandero, who had been deposed by the junta, and reorganized the administration from top to bottom. His overall situation, however, was rapidly deteriorating, for Cabrera found himself in a threadbare and penniless Carlist capital. There were no arms or munitions; there was scarcely an army. Above all, there was no money. General Segarra, provisional commander of Catalonia's Carlist forces, had foreseen Cabrera's animosity and deserted to the enemy a few days before his arrival in Berga.

Catastrophe was inevitable. Espartero, ensconced in his new headquarters in Manresa, collected a formidable army that included the finest liberal generals and awaited a propitious moment to attack. Berga could not possibly resist such an onslaught. Those civilians who were politically compromised began their exodus toward the frontier—some for supposed reasons of health, others on fictitious errands. Cabrera, who harbored no illusions about the real situation, recognized that only those useful in war should remain in Carlist territory and, wishing to save his sisters from the perils of captivity, had them taken in disguise to Perpinyà.

The Count of Morella had not worsened physically, but he suffered from acute depression. Before disaster struck, he told himself, he must find the Owl. This thought both fortified and dismayed him. To hide the vampire's marks, he wore a white silk kerchief around his neck.

Antoni de Montpalau, with Cabrera's approval, set up an office on Holy Christ Street and tried to locate the undead. He organized a network of spies throughout the district, offering a highly publicized reward of fifty *rals* in cash to anyone who led them to the Owl. Among the dissolved junta's papers, he found a letter that caught his eye and clarified several points. It was obviously from the Owl, since it was signed with his name, and the geographical details in his mysterious plan to annihilate Cabrera led Montpalau to conclude that he was near Berga. But where? That was what our naturalist, with scientific precision, sought to ascertain.

In the margin, in Torrebadella's hand, our hero read: "Refused," and beneath it, underlined in the same red pencil: "Mad!" This plunged him into thought, for the Owl, rebuffed on all sides while his enemies—to coin a phrase—were treading on his heels, might be desperate enough to commit some rash act that would lead to his discovery. It all seemed quite plausible.

He decided to wait. One day, as he was recalling his beloved Agnès, Josep Solanes, the veterinarian in charge of the Carlist cavalry, entered the office and said, "I don't know what to do! Some mysterious illness has infected our horses. I can't understand what's wrong with them. They just lie there, slowly dying."

Montpalau replied that it wasn't his specialty and he was sorry to say he could be of no use. That night, however, he consulted a celebrated treatise on horses that he found in the junta's library and that began in this curious fashion:

"The presaunte booke treateth of ways to breake horses and

reyse coltes and how said coltes shoulde be trayned in theyre firste five years and howwe a knighte shoulde accustomme them to spurres and howwe he shoulde sitte in hys saddle and holde hys legges, feete and bodye, and likewyse this booke treateth of horses' coates, tails and mouthes and the bridles they requyre in warfare and the illes and maladies that may befalle them and causes of the same and what a knighte shoulde gyv hys horse to eate and drinke and how fisicks shoulde treate their ailments. This booke was writ by Bernat de Cases, domicyled in the city of Girona, in the service of Hys Most Excellaunt and Christian Majesty King Ferdinand, of blessed reigne and immortalle fame, lorde of Aragon, Castile, the Balearic Isles, the two Sicilies and Jerusalem. And the aforesaide Bernat de Cases, seeing the King of Fraunce beginne to make warre upon our king and the peace and prosperyte that derive from skillfulle cavalry, hath begunne the presaunt booke in the monthe of Aprille, one thousande four hundredde and ninety-six, in whiche a royalle parliamaunt met in Tortosa. I ask alle who reade this tome and understaunde it to correct any errors they finde herein regarding horses, warfare, and the curing of ailments."

In regard to the illnesses that afflict horses, Cases offered an infallible remedy: "Thou shalt seize the horse's righte eer and make the signe of the crosse thryce, saying: 'Quando xpus natus fuit omnis dolor fugatus fuit, fuge dolor, fuge langor quia xpus te persequitur.' This thou muste repeat three tymes, making the signe of the crosse thryce in honour of the Holy Trinity, and the horse will surely be cured."

Montpalau laughed at such pseudo-scientific quackery, whose origin lay in the superstitious ignorance that rational spirits energetically rejected, and he puzzled over the horses' mysterious illness.

On the morrow he went to inspect them, accompanied by the gloomy chief veterinarian. As they entered the stable, he was startled by a strong smell of sulfur.

Montpalau pulled a cross from his pocket and opened a small box of garlic cloves that he always carried. Brandishing these arms and followed by the astonished veterinarian, he penetrated the stable's lugubrious darkness.

"Be careful," Montpalau said. "Stick close by my side."

Good advice, for a dreadful scream greeted our hero's words. It was at once a howl of rage and a despairing lament. Something exploded at the back of the stable, and an entire wall noisily collapsed. The two men were literally buried in debris. They couldn't see a thing.

The explosion brought Isidre de Novau and Amadeu running, along with two guards who, with great efforts, extracted Montpalau and the veterinarian, half-unconscious, from the rubble.

After sipping a highly efficacious cordial, Montpalau, followed by his friends and assistants, again entered the stable. The dust had settled, and they could see clearly.

Just as he had feared! The horses lay there, sadly staring into space, with two tiny holes in each bloodless neck.

Montpalau immediately initiated his Balkan treatment. They had to ensure that those horses did not become vampires. They would try the garlic method, which had often worked so well.

Isidre de Novau, who had been examining the horses, took his pipe from his mouth and said, "Too late. They've just died."

And in fact, they had all passed away at the same instant. Montpalau was horrified by the prospect of two hundred vampire-horses galloping apocalyptically through the night. How tragic and grotesque! But such an abomination would not occur! They had one recourse left: destruction! Destruction, which would also be a liberation.

There was no alternative. That afternoon, before the sun set, they decapitated the horses one by one and filled their mouths with Liliaceae. Then they drove wooden stakes through their hearts. The spell was broken.

Montpalau, ever tactful, made those present swear not to breathe a word of what they had seen to Cabrera. It would have been a fatal blow.

The chief veterinarian reported an epidemic of galloping diarrhea.

5

The Final Investigation

THE soil, intensely ocher, without a blade of grass, parched and desolate, formed a nightmarish landscape of slopes eroded by wind and rain. The route was safe, however, as long as he avoided all settlements. He left Calaceit and Alcanyís behind him and near Codonyeda, heading south, he veered left. It was a bleak area. He found an isolated hermitage with a kind of courtyard inside it, dedicated to the Virgin of Montserrat, and there he ate a piece of bread. Then he headed south again.

Prince Lichnowsky spent the night in a shed. Before daybreak, he set out with his cart. When the sun rose, he spied Morella in the distance. He donned his red beret and uniform covered with glittering medals. He mounted his steed, leaving his cart in a hollow, and set off at a trot for Morella. A few peasants stared at him in surprise.

The road swerved sharply, passed beneath one of the aqueduct's arches, and then made straight for a big fortified gate. Ah, Cabrera, dear old friend! He recalled their advance on Madrid under Charles V, their adventures, and the day he had saved his life.

Suddenly he noticed clumps of dirt flying up ahead of him. He had no time to think. He heard dull, quick shots just as he instinctively hunched over and turned his horse. He took cover behind one of the aqueduct's columns while a bullet ricocheted off the stone, a foot from his head. Then he peered out cautiously.

The queen's flag fluttered on the castle's highest tower. He heard a bugle and saw government uniforms. God in Heaven! What had happened? But there was no time to inquire. He had to escape before a patrol came after him.

On his right, there was a gully full of flowering heather. He spurred his mount and leapt, keeping his eyes shut and feeling Death right behind him. The sky, however, was a bright, indifferent blue. He landed safely.

Beyond the fields, Lichnowsky galloped furiously across the plain. The sky was like a mirror absurdly shattered into a thousand pieces. Everything, including life itself, was absurd. Unexpectedly, a frog croaked.

While the prince fled like a stag toward Catalonia, our hero Antoni de Montpalau, one day after the Owl's assault on the Carlist stables, led his inseparable assistants on a tour of the district.

Their first stop was a shrine called Santa Maria de Queralt, from which they contemplated a marvelous panorama below them. On their descent, they passed through a wood where, without searching, they found a multitude of delicious wild mushrooms.

In Pedret, still seeking an abandoned crypt, they discovered a most interesting but almost ruined village church. The light from their candles revealed some enigmatic, fascinating, but terrifying primitive paintings in the apse. The hands on the cross-eyed figures dressed in tunics seemed disjointed. It was a strange find. As far as Montpalau could recall, no one—not even Father Caresmar—had ever mentioned the place. He would tell the priest and the philologist in the marquis's discussion group about it.

Still pursuing their goal, they visited the monastery at Sant Salvador de la Bellera, where they learned that Espartero was leading a large army toward Berga. They dined on chicken with peppers, onions, and tomatoes—a sensational dish—at a farmhouse. Rising to their feet, they toasted the Owl's capture and the liberals' final victory.

At the monastery, Montpalau chanced to meet a young,

enormously erudite student from Barcelona who was collecting materials—undaunted by the perils of war—for a book about folk legends. His name was Milà i Fontanals, and he told them some extraordinary tales. He didn't know much about vampires, but he was an expert on normal ghosts, of whom there were many with sharply defined personalities in Catalan folklore. He was especially brilliant in his comments on the Evil Hunter and his pack of dogs ranging defiantly over the rooftops. He also mentioned the Devil's appearances in the form of a he-goat with blazing eyes.

The young student told one particularly intriguing story about a ghost, Count Arnau, whose area of operations included Ripoll, Sant Joan de les Abadesses, and Castellar de N'Hug, with incursions into such districts as Prades and Siurana. Illustrious and magically suggestive names appeared, like Mataplana—the little troubadour court—or Gombèn, with its ruined castles and abandoned crypts.

Montpalau pondered this information. He seemed to perceive a certain vampirelike analogy in those ghosts the young student had mentioned. The abandoned crypts interested him greatly.

Milà i Fontanals also said that past Culobre, on the way from Montgrony to Camps, in a cave called The Slit, he had found a stone a yard high hearing the imprints of a horse's hoof and a lady's shoe: the former from Count Arnau's steed and the latter from Adalaisa, the abbess.

In Banyuts Gorge, he had jotted down the following verses:

Had Count Arnau not renounced Our Lord,
The Llobregat's waters we still would ford.

The meaning was obscure, probably because the lines formed part of some long-lost ballad. In any case, someone should attempt to reconstruct the text.

After taking their leave of young Milà i Fontanals, our friends returned to Berga, where sensational news awaited them:

The Duke of Victory and his host had moved their headquarters to Casserres, and an attack on the Carlist town was imminent. Montpalau realized that the war was virtually over.

Berga was in an uproar. Soldiers rushed to and fro, preparing defenses and constructing outworks. Cabrera, very excited, paced about like a caged tiger. He told Montpalau, "It's finished. All that remains is our honor, but if you bear me any affection, do not forget the Owl."

Montpalau assured the general that the evidence he had gathered made the vampire's capture inevitable. It was a matter of hours.

As he left the Count of Morella, an orderly handed him a letter. He thanked him and slipped it into his pocket.

6

The Letter

O N C E Montpalau was in his room, he took off his frock coat, carefully hung it in a wardrobe, filled a basin with water, and scrubbed his hands. Then he rinsed his face and, once it was dry, rubbed his hair vigorously with cologne.

It was hot. Some bottles stood on his chest of drawers. He poured himself a glass of sherry and lit a cigar. Then he pulled the letter from his pocket and, sitting near the oil lamp, opened the envelope. It read:

Dear Sir:

I trust that your powers of deduction will quickly lead you to identify the author of this letter. Alas, you are not mistaken. I am the sadly déclassé Onofre de Dip, commonly known by a dreadful name that I refuse to utter.

I know my hour is drawing nigh, though I suppose that I could forestall the end and I certainly possess the means to do so. I trust that, being a gentleman, you will believe me. I cannot escape my fate, but by means of my magical powers I could, if I wished, prolong this grisly game of cat and mouse. But I have no desire to do so.

My sole purpose in writing this letter is to make you see beyond that abominable and diabolical being created by the popular imagination. I am like a horse hitched to a wagon, longing for a freedom it can scarcely recall. I wander through the world weeping bitter tears.

The Letter

You know my story, but only the part found in official documents—accurate, to be sure, but by no means complete, as it ignores the man who still resides within me. Beneath the satanic appearance circumstances often force me to adopt, in a hidden corner of my soul, I, Onofre de Dip, still persist—the same as before, the same as ever, filled with love for my country and its people, breathing this land's pure air, tearful when I hear some song remembered from my childhood.

What did you expect? Things are never as simple as they seem. When the cunning and beautiful Duchess Meczyr, taking advantage of my shameless lust, turned me into a cursed being, my feelings, once the first shock had passed, were resigned if not joyful. I confess my error. To be able to fly, to turn into any one of a large though limited number of beasts, the incomparable sensation of conjuring up the weather, the thousand and one small and terrifying benefits of my new state, dazzled one as young and inexperienced as I. No mortal can know the exquisite pleasure that tingles in the blood when one turns into an elephant, for example, or—in the opposite direction—an ant.

For seven hundred years I was a corpse's illegitimate consort. Perhaps happily, as I said, at the start, forgetting that I myself was a corpse. I interrupted my long stays in the Carpathians with fleeting visits to Pratdip, where I was born and have—or had—my estates. I believe my intermittent sojourns proved memorable. People still fear me.

But as years passed, something occurred in the depths of my being. The excitement of discovery and the lustful possession of the duchess's eternally young body dissipated. I began to long for my former human state and to weary of this hideous existence. I nearly went mad.

Then the torments began, nor have they yet ceased.

159

Though I still appear young, in reality I am seven hundred years old, disillusioned and bored, craving peace and peace alone. I am horrified by my constant need for blood and can never forget the indescribable looks in my victims' eyes. How cruel is my predicament! For despite everything, I am cursed with a need that I can neither deny nor resist.

The duchess died. Really and truly. She was beheaded and mutilated in a quaint—shall we say—rite. The prophecy's fulfillment began; for once Meczyr Castle had been ransacked, burnt, and purged, my sole haven was Pratdip. I therefore returned—definitively this time—to my native land, knowing full well what awaited me. Impelled by the instinct of self-preservation, I managed to stave off the annihilation of my malevolent nature. This explains the diabolical beasts you have repeatedly seen, as well as several other refinements. Likewise, it explains my adoption of a new personality designed to throw you off the scent. I refer, of course, to the Carlist guerrilla known as the Owl, a tragic and terrible masquerade. Given that I needed some disguise, I chose one that was both heroic and in keeping with my authoritarian and absolutist beliefs.

Of course it was all in vain. What is written is written. Now that my final hour has struck, I only wish to rest. Surely I deserve it after living seven hundred years without living: that is, without sleeping normally, without catching a cold, without tasting a delicious morsel of food, without fondling a baby. At least now I can hope for eternal peace and God's forgiveness.

To this end and in order to spare you further efforts, I solemnly promise that tomorrow, from dawn to dusk, I shall rest in the crypt beneath the castle at Mataplana, whose former owner was a close friend of mine. Have no fear but rather persist in your endeavors. Give me the peace I so desire. No man can escape his fate; what is written is written.

I ask only one favor: Do not subject me to the hideous butchery prescribed by legend. It would be too much for me to bear at my advanced age. Instead, I beg you to employ another formula, less well known, perhaps, but as effective and far more humane: exorcism, accompanied by the song:

> With sun and moon he doth sleep.
> Into his shroud he shall creep,
> In his grave 'neath the earth so deep.

It will put an end to my abominable existence.

I should only like to add, before closing this letter, that surprisingly enough, I bear you great good will. I comprehend your motives, deem them just, and admire the love of science that has brought you such honor. May you enjoy the happiness you so richly deserve.

Your obedient servant,
Onofre de Dip

Deeply stirred by this letter, Antoni de Montpalau sensed the vampire's human presence for the first time. He felt compassion for that miserable and tragic being, Onofre de Dip. He sat there for a moment, thinking.

Several hours later, he met secretly with Cabrera. The two of them spoke together for a long time, locked in the commander's office. The orderlies looked very crestfallen. At times they were startled by the sound of ringing bells. When the two men emerged, Cabrera beamed with optimism, though his face had not lost its vampirelike pallor. He adjusted the kerchief around his neck and inhaled the fragrance of a wild garlic flower.

The sound of rustling leaves could be heard. The *Aurea picuda*—so gentle, unnoticed, and shy—emerged from its hiding place beyond the reach of crass and treacherous humanity. It preened its new and shiny feathers. Then it began to sing an inaudible song of peace, love, and justice.

Montpalau penned a long letter to Father Matons—a letter filled not only with scientific enthusiasm but with meditations on charity and love for one's neighbor. That is, he wrote with both his heart and his mind. He asked a great favor, not devoid of risks but urgent and noble in its purposes. There was no time to spare. He was certain that he needed to say no more.

Amadeu set out that evening—disguised as a peasant woman to avoid troublesome questions—for Barcelona with Antoni de Montpalau's letter. He rode on the crupper of a notion peddler's horse. The man had been well paid for his services. The night was dark and ominous.

7

The Fall of Berga

THIS was a fateful day for what remained of the Carlist forces. The liberal troops began to take up positions around the city. Their triumph was nearly complete. Cabrera officially freed Antoni de Montpalau, trusting, however, that he would not desist until he had completed the task before him. Montpalau, followed by his cousin Isidre de Novau, left Berga and set out for Pobla de Lillet. When they had gone several miles, they stopped in a place that offered an excellent view of the battle.

The clash was epic in its grandeur. To better inform our readers, we shall copy the description of this remarkable event from *Espartero's Life and Times*, which, despite its violent attacks on the Count of Morella—quite natural, to be sure, in an anti-Carlist work—gives far more details than *Cabrera's Life and Times*, which—as is also quite natural—tries to gloss over his defeat:

"Once our troops had completed their preparations, they set out, led by the Duke of Victory, from their headquarters in Casserres on July fourth. Seeing the numerous bastions behind which the Carlists had taken cover, prepared to resist to the bitter end and egged on by their commander Cabrera with pleas, threats, and exhortations, the Duke of Victory summoned the Count of Belascoain, whose courage he valued highly, and ordered him to lead the attack with the first division, while the brigade of royal provincial guards remained in reserve. Undaunted by the foe's strong positions and the obstacles in his path, the intrepid count prepared to carry out Espartero's orders, but as he did so, the Carlists opened fire from Nuet Hill, causing some casualties among the constitutionalist ranks. The count and his troops had reached a farmhouse called Creu de la Penya. Here he marshaled his forces and ordered the first brigade and the hussars to press forward, keeping a close watch on an enemy squadron to their left. One need scarcely add that the count was in an awkward position, exposed as he was to enemy fire. Unafraid, the valiant commander who directed this perilous maneuver told his troops to return the Carlists' fire energetically, protecting those who struggled to mount their artillery on the hillside. The Carlists' efforts proved vain, for once the guns were ready they began to fire, permitting the queen's forces to advance swiftly and enthusiastically to our foes' first line of defense. The Carlists, obliged to flee this valiant onslaught, took refuge behind their second line of defense. Here too, however, they were boldly attacked and a struggle began that, though brief, was bloody and violent.

"The queen's battalions advanced bravely under their general, while the dreaded Cabrera, not wishing to be outdone by his heroic adversary, roared like a lion and ran to and fro, urging his men to return our fire and to sow death among the attackers. Both sides fought furiously, but the Count of Belascoain, feeling that this stalemate had lasted long enough, led some of his officers, his personal guard, and a few of Espartero's cavalry in a desperate assault on Nuet Hill. They thus decided the battle with their bayonets, forcing the Carlists to abandon their positions. Most of those the queen's general led were killed or wounded, and he had to abandon his steed, which had been struck by four bullets, nor was it the first he had lost in that gory battle. Cabrera, despairing at this setback and aware that all was lost, dashed about like a raging beast, throwing himself into the fray wherever it was thickest, seeking victims on whom he might vent his fury or a bullet that would end his life and save his honor. [Note: this, however, is untrue, for there was still the vampire to attend to.]

Forgetting his illness in a fit of feverish activity, he stiffened the Carlists' resolve, thus making the liberals' triumph all the more remarkable and adding luster to the glory with which they covered themselves that day.

"Thanks to the Count of Belascoain's brilliance, not only were the three above-mentioned redoubts occupied but also all the other defenses around Berga and finally the city itself, from which Cabrera, still unbowed, ordered his men to retreat. Two Carlist companies, however, disobeyed his orders and continued to fire upon our men from some fields outside the walls. Then the battle-hardened Count of Belascoain, vexed by their audacity, sallied forth with his cavalry and, covered by our marksmen, charged the companies, which, when they sought to flee, found themselves surrounded and were quickly captured. Masters of Berga, its castle, and its defenses, the queen's soldiers discovered huge supplies of ammunition, rifles, and gunpowder, as well as an armory, a depot, a forge, and sixteen guns of varying calibers that Cabrera had been unable to remove or spike. In his flight from Berga, the last bastion of Carlism, Cabrera was followed by many of the city's inhabitants—some out of sympathy and others moved by fear of the conquering army and no doubt troubled by their consciences, which warned them that retribution was at hand for the disasters they had caused through their criminal connivance.

"Undaunted by this battle, in which apart from the dead and wounded, they had lost two of their best companies, the Carlists continued to fire as though they still hoped to retake the city. In vain their bugles sounded the retreat, for those fanatics persisted until Cabrera himself addressed his troops, saying, 'Come on, boys, it's time to go.' They withdrew at nightfall. The cursed star that for so long had favored Cabrera set at last, and he retreated with two battalions from Tortosa, three from Móra, five from Aragon, and some Catalan forces led by Father Tristany, including Pep de l'Oli's battalion. Those defending the shrine at L'Hort, armed with six cannon, continued to fire, seeking to cover their retreating comrades and distract the queen's troops, but upon beholding the Count of Belascoain's dreaded lance, they abandoned their positions, which he occupied without resistance. Cabrera's army had been routed and demoralized. Desertions, which had been numerous for some time, now multiplied, while the officers turned a blind eye to their fleeing men, knowing as they did that Carlism could not long endure. What remained of the army dispersed that evening to various villages in the Pyrenees, four or five leagues from Berga."

Charles V's partisans had reached the end of the line. Antoni de Montpalau and his cousin, having watched the battle, spurred their mounts and set out for Castellar de N'Hug, where they had arranged to meet the defeated general. As soon as day broke and Amadeu returned from his mission, they would head for Mataplana, free Cabrera, and bring peace to the Dip.

Evening thickened about our friends. A real owl hooted, perched in a leafy oak tree. They heard some brook's invisible and crystalline waters. A breeze from the Pyrenees cooled the Barcelonans' feverish brows. The earth stirred with a thousand mysterious rustlings.

Meanwhile Prince Lichnowsky, galloping through a cloud of dust two hours from Cervera, tried to catch up with the Carlist forces he expected to find in Berga. His heart pounded as he rode, still marveling at his narrow escape.

From time to time, as he skirted a village, he heard gunfire behind him. Seeking a safe haven, Prince Lichnowsky galloped like the wind. He was filthy and would have given anything for a glass of water. Naturally, he had no notion of what had occurred in Berga.

8

Onofre de Dip Finds Peace

Dawn broke amid somber, low-lying clouds. A strong
north wind blew, forcing the defeated troops, camped
near Castellar de N'Hug, to pull their capes tightly around them.
The village's rustic inhabitants stared fearfully at those soldiers
in search of shelter. There were long faces all around, and an
infinite sadness weighed upon them. The army's discipline had
disintegrated, and the men mingled with their officers, wander-
ing idly here and there.

Seated around a crude table at an inn, the Count of Morella,
Montpalau, and Isidre drank hot coffee. Cabrera looked exhausted; the previous day's events had left their mark on him.
Feeling a chill, he clutched the top of his cape. It was clear that
the Count of Morella was consumed by fever.

Later that morning, Amadeu and Father Matons arrived.
They also looked exhausted—and especially Amadeu—after
traveling for two days without pause. Montpalau and Matons
embraced. The priest spoke with great tact and delicacy, and
his face beamed with an innate goodness that soothed and cheered
his listeners. Montpalau introduced him to those present. Cabrera
could scarcely conceal his emotion. Everyone felt a bit feverish
in that atmosphere of alert, expectant tension. They were all
thinking of what they were about to do and the unique experience that awaited them. The spell would at last be broken. At
midday they rode forth in single file from Castellar de N'Hug:
Cabrera, Father Matons, Montpalau, Novau, and Amadeu. The
only paths leading to Mataplana were trails used by shepherds.

The landscape, stark and wild, abounded in mountain flora. Montpalau discreetly collected a few herbs, including an extremely rare specimen of *Matricaria chamomilla*.

The path climbed to great heights and then descended through dark valleys shaded by fir trees. They found small, icy waterfalls and deep, sinister gorges. Though it was summer, their ears reddened in the chilly air. They followed the path, occasionally spying herds of sheep cropping the gray, stunted weeds. A few ravens circled overhead.

They reached Maians, a farmhouse on the plateau known as La Pera or L'Espluga. Here they began another steep descent along a wooded slope that ended in a majestic hollow. At one end of the hollow, perched on a craggy hill, stood the famous Mataplana Castle, not far from Banyuts Gorge.

As they started down, Amadeu and Novau had to cross their arms to make a seat for Cabrera, who nearly fainted when he beheld the castle. Between his exhaustion and the sight of that cursed spot, the Count of Morella, whose nerves were usually so steely, felt that he could go no farther and had to ask the Barcelonans for help. He was as white as a sheet, and his brow was beaded with sweat.

Ahead of them loomed the ruined castle and the silhouetted chapel of Sant Joan de Mata. Lightning snaked across the sky, followed by a mighty clap of thunder.

Father Matons drew forth his breviary and draped his stole around his neck. His companions fingered their crosses and felt for the garlic in their pockets. Cabrera had aged considerably.

Darkness began to fall as the sun sank behind the mountains. The long-awaited moment was at hand. It was now or never. Montpalau pointed to the castle door, and our friends silently made their way thither. As they entered, they heard a long, grief-stricken howl, as though a wolf were lost in the woods behind them. Their hair stood on end and they halted, terrified, gazing at one another questioningly.

It only lasted a moment, for Montpalau, knowing that night

would soon fall, took a few steps forward by himself. This broke the spell, and the others followed suit.

Lighting their lanterns, they went down the steps leading to the crypt. Stone tombs lined the walls, resting on ancient sculpted corbels. Everywhere there were inscriptions in indecipherable Latin. Huge cobwebs covered the crypt's arching vault.

As they had expected, a large open tomb stood in the middle. Prepared for anything, they approached it, holding their garlic aloft. In the tomb, their astonished eyes beheld the huge and vigorous body of His Majesty's former ambassador, Onofre de Dip. He was wrapped in a cape, and his face was ruddy. His expression was stern, curiously noble, and tinged with grief.

The sun was about to set. Matons stepped forward and solemnly recited his prayers. A strange sound issued from that prostrate body. When the priest had finished, Montpalau uttered the magic formula:

> "With sun and moon he doth sleep.
> Into his shroud he shall creep,
> In his grave 'neath the earth so deep."

Then something truly amazing occurred. A great peace transformed the vampire's face, and his lips parted in a smile. His skin slowly wrinkled and lost its freshness, darkening and becoming like that of a mummy. It was a horrible but reassuring sight. Bone and cartilage appeared. Everything gradually withered away till only dust remained.

Simultaneously, they all turned toward the Count of Morella. As though by enchantment—and indeed, that's what it was—he felt his vitality return, and his face regained its color. Upon examining him, Montpalau saw that those two sores had disappeared.

Falling to their knees, they uttered heartfelt prayers for the soul of the deceased and in thanks for the favors God had granted them. Their previous tension had given way to a miraculous serenity. Everything was different, and their hearts pounded with joy.

A cool breeze caressed their faces as they emerged from the crypt after sealing Onofre de Dip's last resting place. Those threatening clouds had vanished, and the setting sun tinted the bluish horizon.

Banyuts Gorge glowed with a phosphorescent light that quickly faded away.

Unexpectedly, in a strange vision outlined against the sky, they saw Prince Lichnowsky, galloping away from Berga. His face reflected horror and consternation. He rode toward Castellar de N'Hug, with the Furies close behind him.

9

An End to Heroism

WHEN the Count of Morella returned to Castellar de N'Hug, he was met by his officers Ferran Pineda and Lluís Adell, who had gone to negotiate with General Castellane at the French border. They would be admitted to France under the following conditions: First, all generals, officers, and troops would be initially transported to places chosen by the French government, which would grant them political asylum; second, they would be welcomed, treated, and respected as refugees; third, they would have the right to reside in France or continue on to other destinations of their choosing; fourth, the troops would surrender their arms and horses, except those personally owned by the generals and officers.

Having considered these points, Cabrera summoned his officers and said, "Comrades in arms, I began this war with fifteen men, only half of whom possessed rifles. Now, however, I see no further hope of victory. Given the circumstances, I believe that continuing the struggle would only cause useless bloodshed. I am convinced that my duty is to lead you safely to France, as the king has not authorized me to negotiate with our enemies. I thank you, in his name and still more in my own, for your loyalty and courage throughout this campaign. If anyone thinks that the battle is not yet lost, I give him leave to continue in whatever fashion he desires. I feel that I have done my duty; should you wish to condemn me, now is the time. Here I stand; we are still on Catalan soil. I want to be judged not as a general but as a simple volunteer, for I prefer death to ignominy."

Silence greeted the commander's first few words. By the time he had finished, all his officers were weeping. Forcadell and Llagostera were the most deeply affected, as they had fought in all their heroic leader's campaigns.

Montpalau witnessed this pathetic scene and, despite his liberal convictions, he was filled with sadness. He stepped out into the cold night air. The stars shone brilliantly overhead. Soon Novau joined him, silently smoking his pipe.

"It's over; everything must come to an end. There are no more mysteries to unravel. You, Novau, will again set sail for Malta, while I return to my plants and Leyden jars. Ten years from now, we shall vaguely recall this adventure, but never again shall we see another like it."

Montpalau spoke bitterly. A shooting star plummeted earthward. Novau replied, "People will think we're crazy if we tell them the truth. You, in particular, will have to lie to maintain your scientific reputation. A priest's corroboration won't do you much good."

He chortled and spat into a clump of gorse.

"Such is life," he added.

They had been leaning against a wall. Someone emerged and emptied a bucket of dirty water. They returned to the inn, where everyone was preparing to set out. The floor was strewn with pieces of paper and tin cans. The main hall was deserted.

A few minutes later, they were riding toward France. Montpalau had decided to go as far as the border, where the three inseparable friends and Father Matons would take their leave of Cabrera.

It was three o'clock in the morning. The army followed behind them, except for Tristany's guerrillas, who had decided to fight on in Catalonia. Their footsteps echoed in the icy night. The trek seemed interminable. The French town of Palau's lights twinkled in the distance.

As dawn began to break, they spied a battalion of mounted

gendarmes awaiting them in accord with their agreement. Everything was diffuse and unreal, as though glimpsed in a dream, and the lights slowly took on a grainy and nacreous texture. The gendarmes waited, solemn and still.

Montpalau rode beside the Count of Morella. As they approached, they saw the commissary tugging at his horse's reins. He asked, "Which of you is General Cabrera?"

"At your service," Cabrera replied as he dismounted. Then he turned to Montpalau with tears streaming down his cheeks. The two men embraced.

"I can never repay you!" Cabrera exclaimed. "I know neither what fate holds in store for me nor where I shall be tomorrow, nor do I know what will become of this wretched land of ours. But whatever happens and wherever I may go, do not forget that I consider you my brother."

Then he removed his saber and handed it to Montpalau, who remained silent.

"Take this saber as a token of my esteem. As you can see, I have nothing else to offer and it is my most prized possession. Take it."

"Thank you, general," Montpalau replied, looking away to hide his tears.

Gripping the young naturalist's arm, Cabrera muttered, "You're a damn good liberal." And smiling, he added, "The only one I ever met."

Then he looked at the French commissary and said, "I'm ready."

At that moment, they heard hoofbeats swiftly approaching. They all turned around. Half fainting, Prince Lichnowsky appeared with barely enough strength to halt just before he reached the border. Then he slipped from his saddle, while the men rushed to aid him.

The sun had risen. Wisps of smoke rose from Palau's chimneys. The Carlist army entered France.

Very slowly, Montpalau mounted his steed. He glanced at the general's saber. Then he and his friends, who had been waiting, turned back to Spain.

Return to Love

BARCELONA was in a festive mood. News had arrived that the war at last was over. Five days earlier,
the city had feted the queen mother and Isabella II. A week
later, they would welcome the Duke of Victory. Flowers and
violins were the order of the day. The press described these
glorious events in the following terms:

"Their Majesties' entrance, together with their retinue, was
at once solemn and joyous. Many factors combined to create an
atmosphere of grandeur and magnificence—most importantly, our
desire to see the young queen now occupying Saint Ferdinand's
throne, whose preservation cost the nation so many hard sacri-
fices, as well as the pomp and circumstance that always attend a
mighty court. Catalonia's capital welcomed the illustrious travelers at seven on the evening of June thirtieth with rapturous
applause. Soldiers and militiamen lined the route, awaiting a
cannonade that would announce the royal ladies' arrival, while
crowds gathered around the gate through which they would pass.
Before entering the city, however, Their Majesties stopped at a
place called La Creu Coberta and rested for a few minutes in a
pavilion erected in their honor. There they were congratulated
by the authorities and notables who had come to greet them,
kissing their hands and offering them refreshments, which they
sipped as they wandered about the pavilion, accompanied by a
lady-in-waiting and their chief steward. As they left, the city
fathers offered, and Their Majesties accepted, a luxurious and
elegant triumphal coach drawn by eight richly caparisoned horses

and driven by eight splendidly attired coachmen. The royal party was preceded by a squadron of lancers from the National Militia, who later joined the royal horse guards in protecting our guests. Her Grace the Duchess of Victory, the Count of Santa Coloma, and Catalonia's captain general Antoni Van-Halen also accompanied the royal ladies in open carriages.

"Upon reaching a triumphal arch erected at the Boqueria Gate, Their Majesties spied various Barcelonan maidens dressed as nymphs. The procession halted for a moment while the maids sang in chorus, recited poetry, and offered floral wreaths. Doves adorned with multicolored ribbons flew through the air, and shouts of joy sped the royal travelers on their way to the palace, where they watched the troops and national militiamen pass in review. Barcelona's happiness was complete; private citizens vied with one another in bedecking their houses."

Meanwhile, Father Matons, Montpalau, and their friends returned to Barcelona, following the safest and shortest route: the one starting in Ripoll. Field Marshal Jaume Carbó, who commanded Espartero's third army, gave them a tilbury that, while not as elegant as the one they had left at the inn in Camposines, was quite solid and comfortable. General Carbó, who had attended school with Montpalau's father, threw a small party to celebrate their victory. Bottles of French champagne were uncorked amid toasts to the queen's health.

After belching, General Carbó expounded his belief that the queen's reactionary ministers must be done away with. Above all, they had to protect the constitution, enlighten the populace, and raise Spain to the level of other European nations. In brief, they must pay tribute to progress.

Father Matons courteously but sternly replied, "You will permit me to observe that, as history has amply shown, the Church has never faltered in its pastoral mission, and the ills that hang like a curse over our country derive from an unhealthy weakening of faith among the ruling classes."

Insisting that he couldn't agree more, General Carbó ushered his guests into the *fumoir,* where they lit some Cuban cigars. Cordiality reigned supreme, aided by the champagne's gaseous vapors. General Carbó displayed a handsome pistol from his collection. Montpalau's thoughts were elsewhere, for he was dreaming of his Agnès.

General Carbó said goodbye to Antoni Montpalau and his companions by the side of the road to Sant Joan de les Abadesses. They set off toward Vic, the land of aromatic sausages. At the entrance to each village they saw a triumphal arch inscribed with the words "Long live the queen!" and "Long live the constitution!"

Amadeu, so long parted from his profession, excitedly drove the tilbury at top speed. Observing Montpalau's sad countenance, the priest thought it wise to tell their coachman to show more serenity and composure.

They had nearly reached Barcelona. Winking at Novau, Matons told the melancholy naturalist, "First let's go to the Marquis de la Gralla's house. He has a surprise for you."

These words were accompanied by a mighty crack of the whip, gracefully executed by Amadeu, who was grinning from ear to ear.

As they passed Marcus's Chapel on Carders Street, they noticed how festively the shops had been decorated. Their owners strolled about as though it were Sunday, wearing silk hats and smoking cigarettes. To distract our hero, the sage priest re-marked, "Watch your step with Segimon Ferrer, Montpalau. He's a dangerous skeptic."

This observation was quickly embellished by intrepid Ama-deu, who, perhaps influenced by the vocabulary of those soldiers they had left at the border, turned around and said, "Mr. Ferrer is a nincompoop."

They all roared with laughter—except Montpalau, who glowered at his coachman. Amadeu, however, knew how far he could go with his master.

They halted outside the gates to the Marquis de la Gralla's

palace. Footmen wearing wigs and white gloves stood at the entrance. They opened the carriage door, bowed, and helped the travelers out.

At the top of the steps, artistically arranged in order of importance, stood the smiling and excited members of their circle: the marquis, Samsó Corbella, Bartomeu Garriga, Josep Ignasi, and Francesc Avinyó. All except Segimon Ferrer, the skeptic.

Montpalau opened his arms. He held his top hat in one hand.

They surrounded him in a lively demonstration of joy. Everyone spoke at once. They had been informed, yes, they had heard all about it. Amazing, the discovery of the century, incredible, a bombshell! What acumen! What a glorious day for Catalan science!

They escorted him to the reception room, where the divine Chopin had once played the piano. Upon one of the tables stood a gold statue of a *Vampiris diminutus* on a polished mahogany base—a free interpretation of an allegorical bat, executed, with his usual good taste, by Gumersind Cortès of Ferran Street.

"My son," said the marquis, "here you see a small token of our enthusiastic admiration. All our names are on the pedestal. It's solid gold."

Bartomeu Garriga, the philologist, eager to hear more about Montpalau's exploits, shifted impatiently from one foot to the other. He tried to interrupt the marquis.

"The etymological origin of . . ."

"Just a second, Garriga. Don't break my train of thought. All in good time." Then the marquis continued, "And now, my son, we have a special surprise, one I am sure our friend Father Matons has already mentioned."

So saying, the marquis smiled and gestured toward the door. All eyes were fixed upon Montpalau.

"Go ahead. Open it."

With beating heart, Montpalau obeyed. He took a few steps into the next room.

Agnès stood by the window, inhaling a rose's fragrance.

"Agnès," Montpalau whispered, choking on his words.

"Darling Antoni," she tearfully replied.

Our naturalist threw himself at his beloved's feet and kissed her hand.

Agnès smiled.

Far away, the *Aurea picuda* intoned its perfect and inaudible song.

Then there was silence, like the world's noiseless throbbing just before its creation. Nothingness.

Index of Proper Names

Agnès: The Baroness d'Urpí's daughter. Her delicate presence stirred the souls of plants. She grew up in Pratdip, married Antoni de Montpalau, a celebrated nineteenth-century naturalist, and died in 1874.

Alcoverro, Josep: Gandesa's liberal mayor. Unafraid to speak his mind.

Amadeu: Antoni de Montpalau's coachman. Entered the family's service at the age of eight. He was exceptionally loyal to his master, with whom he reminisced, when they were both well into their sixties and suffering from insomnia, about their past adventures. He died, leaving several children, at the age of ninety in a house in Sant Cugat del Vallès that his former master had willed to him.

Ambrose, Saint: Fourth-century saint. Formidable Latinist. Composed "Aeterne rerum conditor" ("Framer of the Earth and Sky").

Ardenya, Martí d': Illustrious naturalist born in Altafulla in the province of Tarragona. Corrected several of Lavoisier's errors.

Arissó, Carles: One of Ramon Cabrera's doctors. Dismissed for faulty diagnosis of his commander's illness. He died consumed by jealousy of Antoni de Montpalau's scientific successes.

Arnes: The last village in Tarragona before entering Aragon. Its town hall resembles a Florentine palace.

Arpiazu the cook: Carlist volunteer who taught a flying reptile to talk. He went mad and died in the town of Zarauz during a thunderstorm.

Aurea picuda: Winged creature of undetermined species. Its song was a pure and inaudible melody. Shy. Strangely devoted to Antoni de Montpalau.

Avinyó i Barba, Francesc: Medical scholar and member of the Marquis de la Gralla's circle. Paid for some refreshments at the Peru Café. Owned a textile mill. Ruined by strikes over the introduction of self-acting mules.

Avutarda geminis: A mysterious beast that fascinated and perplexed naturalists for years. Then it suddenly disappeared from the face of the earth.

Banyuts Gorge: Locus of several legends. It seems that Count Arnau and Adalaisa took refuge there during their idyll. It glowed for a few seconds after Onofre de Dip's death.

Baron de Meer: Barcelonan. As captain general of Catalonia, he distinguished himself in the struggle against Count Charles of Spain. A cultivated man.

Index of Proper Names

Baroness d'Urpí: Agnès's mother and the Marquis de la Gralla's sister. Antoni de Montpalau's mother-in-law. Passed away in 1840.

Baroness of Néziers: Related to Antoni de Montpalau on his mother's side and very close to Aurore Dupin, commonly known as George Sand. She enjoyed reading eighteenth-century pornographic French novels. Mistress of the painter Josep Maria de Martín, a Carlist exile living in Paris.

Bassa, General: General Llauder's second in command. He died tragically, thrown from a window above the Pla del Palau.

Bonaplata, Ramonet: A cretin born into a good family. Had an illegitimate son by Pepeta, the chambermaid.

Borso di Carminati, General: A liberal officer of Italian extraction, as his name suggests. Fought bravely during a siege of Gandesa.

Cabrera, Ramon: Commander of the Carlist armies of Aragon, Valencia, Murcia, and later Catalonia as well. Famed throughout the world for his courage and cunning. Toward the end of the campaign he contracted a strange malady cured by the timely intervention of his friend Antoni de Montpalau. Cabrera later married and settled in London, where he lived surrounded by pedigreed setters.

Calmet, Friar: Specialist in demonology and vampirism. He died in Brittany, kneeling before a wayside cross. His works were published by the Sorbonne.

Cantaluppo, Captain: Aeronaut. Made a trip around the world in eighty days, inspiring Jules Verne's novel of that name.

Carbó, Jaume: A liberal general, envied for his collection of antique weapons. Played an active role in the First Carlist War.

Chamber of Commerce: Barcelonan institution, highly influential in the city's intellectual life.

Charles V: The Carlist pretender.

Colonna d'Este, Prince: A Roman aristocrat. He wore flowered robes and adored art. Famed for his seductions. One day, a Japanese friend presented him with a geisha. Close friend of Prince Lichnowsky, whom he introduced to fair Matilde de Ferrari. Bored with life, he committed suicide in the early hours of November 7, 1847.

The Commercial Echo
The Constitutionalist
The National Guard
The Steamship
Uproar
The Young Observer

Catalan newspapers of the era. They may be consulted in Barcelona's Municipal Historical Archives.

Cordelles College: A Barcelonan school.

Courreur des Sciences: Widely read scientific publication.

Dead Man's Cave: A cave in the Maestrat. One reaches it by turning south after crossing the Beseit Mountains. The site of some of Antoni de Montpalau's most extraordinary discoveries, including petrifying music, a phenomenon that unfortunately has not been studied further.

Despuig, Cristòfor: Published a curious work entitled *Talks Given in*

Index of Proper Names

the Illustrious City of Tortosa by Sir Cristòfor Despuig. Contains many observations of great interest to naturalists.

Dip, Onofre de: A vampire. During the Carlist Wars he was also known as the Owl. Knighted by King James I, he fell in love with Duchess Meczyr, herself a vampire who infected him with her dreadful condition. Lord of Pratdip. Found peace at last, through Antoni de Montpalau's efforts, after the many vicissitudes recounted in this novel.

Escoda, Francesc: One of Gandesa's most distinguished liberals.

Espartero, General: Responsible for the defeat of Carlism. He was named Duke of Victory, and later of Morella as well. Rather vain. Had some serious conflicts with the regent Maria Cristina. Played a major role in Spanish politics.

Ferrari, Matilde de: Her married name was Matilde Leblanc. Lichnowsky's grand and hopeless passion. A friend of George Sand's.

Ferrer, Segimon: Discoverer of mathematical coagulation. A skeptic with no taste for poetry. He took a dislike to Antoni de Montpalau, whose views he often belittled. Died in Seville of a surfeit of gazpacho. His enemies were many and well deserved.

Ferrery, Juan Manuel: Eminent scientist born in Pasajes de San Juan. Donated Saint Faustina's body, intact and uncorrupted, to his parish church. One day, at a reception held by the King of Bavaria, he uttered the celebrated phrase: "Everything is nothing." Died in Bayonne, France.

Flying Reptile, the: Survivor of prehistoric times. Talked like a parrot. Slow and dreamy, it frightened dogs.

Forcadell, General: Cabrera's second in command. Considered his right-hand man.

Four Nations Inn: Frederic Chopin and George Sand stayed there.

Galvan, Antoni: Liberal physician in Gandesa. Rang a copper bell as he collected the wounded.

Gandesa: Liberal Catalan town. Figures in Galdós's *Episodios nacionales.* Its inhabitants are hot-blooded and hard-working.

Garlic: A highly effective protection against vampires. Of the Liliaceae family. A bulbous plant. Strong flavor.

Garriga, Bartomeu: Member of the Marquis de la Gralla's circle. Philologist. On a youthful trip to Asturias, he met Jovellanos. Peculiar laugh. In his old age he became hard of hearing and used an ear trumpet. Passed away in 1858.

Gil, Pere: Jesuit and naturalist born in Reus. Author of a famous *Natural History of Catalonia.*

Gombrèn: Village near Ripoll. Frequent sightings of Count Arnau. Old people still recite the lines: "Had Count Arnau not renounced Our Lord/ The Llobregat's waters we still would ford."

Hilary of Poitiers, Saint: Wrote poetry in Latin.

Horta de Sant Joan: An extremely picturesque village not far from Gandesa. Immortalized in our time by Picasso's cubist paintings c. 1906. The liberals called it Horta de l'Ebre.

183

Index of Proper Names

Josep Ignasi: The Marquis de la Gralla's heir. Inventor of the pneumatic harp (see below) and the liberal flute. Gifted musician. After coming into his title and inheritance, he moved to Montmartre, where he staged enthusiastically received scientific-cultural shows.

Junta of Berga: Catalonia's Carlist junta, headquartered in Berga. Believed responsible for Count Charles of Spain's death at Coll de Nargó. Issued pompous proclamations.

Laborde, Alexandre de: French traveler who wrote *Voyage pittoresque de l'Espagne* and *Itinéraire descriptif de l'Espagne*. Thorough in his research. Blue eyed. A great lover of mayonnaise.

La Gralla, Marquis de: Barcelonan aristocrat. Member of the Academy of Science. A distinguished scientific circle gathered regularly at his house. A man of good will and great authority. He was researching a study to determine the feasibility of acclimatizing and raising ostriches in Prat de Llobregat. The Baroness d'Urpí's brother, and therefore Agnès's uncle.

Lammark-Boucher et de la Truanderie, Sir: Related to Antoni de Montpalau on his mother's side. Famous botanist. Owned coffee plantations in Haiti. Widowed in 1813.

Leblanc: *See* Ferrari.

Lesseps, Ferdinand: French consul in Barcelona. Solid scientific background. Great future ahead of him.

Liberty Café: In Gràcia. A gathering place for progressives. The owner, Vicentet, hailed from Sant Sadurní and had a strange and nefarious habit of spoiling the wine he was fermenting.

Lichnowsky, Prince: Carlist volunteer related to the German imperial family. Very crafty. Hopelessly in love with Matilde de Ferrari. Played the piccolo with great delicacy. A tremendous success with women, he possessed a most refined sensibility. Came to a tragic end.

Llagostera, General: Another of Cabrera's aides. Valiant. Knew how to endure hardship.

Madoz y Fontaneda: Naturalist residing in Seville. Consulted frequently with American naturalists. An authority on flying mammals, he found—after a laborious search—an amphibious lizard's egg. One night, when he was staying at an inn in Madrid, a valuable talking watch was stolen from his room. This event in turn led to a bitter dispute with the minister of justice.

Magrinyà i Sunyer, Antoni: Ex-president of Tarragona's provincial deputation. Polymath. Wrote a history of the sieges of Gandesa, which that city's council resolved to publish. Decision postponed indefinitely due to lack of funds.

Majorcan, The: Vessel on which George Sand and Chopin sailed to Majorca.

Mani, Oriol: Gandesan liberal volunteer.

Marina, Saint: Shrine near Pratdip. Scenes of great devotion. Multitudinous processions.

Martí, Joan: One of Cabrera's incompetent doctors.

Mas, Bernat: Eminent botanist.

Index of Proper Names

Mataplana Castle: Hug de Mataplana's old troubadour court. Onofre de Dip, the undead, found peace in its crypt. Currently in ruins. Picturesque spot.

Matons, Pasqual: Liberal priest and member of the Marquis de la Gralla's circle. Composed poetry in his spare time and compiled a bibliography of early Catalan authors. He ended his life as Bishop of Murcia. Wrote an ode to progress in Latin, published in *The Steamship*.

Meczyr, Duchess: Undead. A Hungarian beauty. Beheaded and quartered. Transmitted her condition to Onofre de Dip.

Milà i Fontanals, Manuel: Scholar who later taught Menéndez y Pelayo. Strong influence on the nineteenth-century Catalan revival.

Minosca, Peret: Inhabitant of Pratdip. One of the vampire's victims.

Moles, Enriqueta: Another victim of the vampire.

Montpalau, Antoni de: Exceptionally brilliant scientist. Member of the Academy of Science. A rationalist in his youth, he later declared that he had discovered poetry through three things: love, mystery, and adventure. Hero of this novel. Died of a heart attack in Amsterdam.

Morella: Capital of the Maestrat. Magnificent cathedral guarded by choleric priests.

Navarro, Rafael: Gunner. Liberal defender of Gandesa.

Niccolò: A hair-raising fish, the Genoese *pesce cola*.

Novau, Isidre de: Sea captain. Antoni de Montpalau's cousin and inseparable companion on many an adventure. Came to a strange end: As his vessel approached Malta, he sighted the terrifying *pesce cola* for the second time. After locking himself in his cabin, he vanished without a trace, obliging his first mate to take charge of the ship. He willed his fortune to Antoni de Montpalau.

Nuñez, Leopoldo: Another of the vampire's victims. Castilian. Bailiff by trade.

Ocaña, Manuel: Notary. Liberal defender of Gandesa. Fond of polkas.

O'Donnell, General: One of the queen's best. Related to the Carlist Colonel O'Donnell, slain by the mob in Barcelona.

Otorrinus fantasticus: An indescribable beast.

Owl, the: *See* Onofre de Dip.

Pascual, Josep Maria: Jurist. Liberal defender of Gandesa.

Pep de l'Oli: Carlist guerrilla. Did the best he could.

Peru Café: A Barcelonan café. George Sand enjoyed some refreshments there in the company of the Marquis de la Gralla's circle.

Peuderrata, Magí: Mayor of Pratdip. Extremely quick to spot traces of hares and partridges. After his wife's death he moved to Barcelona, where he managed a brothel. Sentenced to the galleys, he died at the entrance to Maó's harbor.

Piper of the Llobregat: Pen name of Joaquim Rubió i Ors, highly influential in the nineteenth-century Catalan renaissance. His verses were famed throughout the land. Founded a dynasty of literary giants.

Plancy, Collin de: Author of treatises on demonology and vampirism. Fond of blondes and brocade. Active in the Inquisition in Cahors.

Index of Proper Names

Pneumatic harp: A musical artifact invented by Josep Ignasi, the Marquis de la Gralla's son. It made a great impression on Chopin during his brief stay in Barcelona.

Pratdip: Village in the province of Tarragona, tyrannized by the Dip. See this novel.

Prim i Prats, Joan: Captain in the queen's army. Played a major role in Spanish politics once he became a general. Crowned Amadeo of Savoy King of Spain. Born in Reus. Assassinated on Turk Street, Madrid, December 30, 1870.

Riera, Narcís: Head of Cordelles School. Delivered speeches in formal Castilian.

Sabater, Matias: Liberal defender of Gandesa.

Sallent, Marquis de: Liberal extremist. Died battling like a lion in a Carlist ambush outside Campdevànol.

Salvador, Jaume: One of Catalan science's founding fathers. Superb botanist. His herbarium is still famous.

Sand, George: Pseudonym of Aurore Dupin. Dressed like a man. Celebrated authoress. Scandalized the Majorcans.

Scolopendra martirialis: Monstrous and horrifying insect. A born killer. Looks like a giant centipede.

Segarra, General: Carlist commander of Catalonia. Member of the Junta of Berga. Deserted to the enemy and issued a famous proclamation in Ripoll, urging his colleagues to surrender.

Simius saltarinus: Leaping monkey. Its fur is preserved with naphthalene.

Sol, Josep: Gandesan merchant. Played an active role in the city's defense.

Solanes, Josep: Cabrera's chief veterinarian. Reported the demise of all his commander's horses due to an epidemic of galloping diarrhea.

Solaní: Carlist guerrilla leader who operated along the Ebre.

Tenies intestinalis: Intestinal parasites in the form of long worms. Blind. Produce a general feeling of malaise in their victims.

Torrebadella, Father: Machiavellian reactionary priest. Briefly headed the Junta of Berga. Personal enemy of Father Matons. He was deposed by Cabrera and found himself obliged to give lessons in applied Machiavellianism during his exile in Grenoble.

Vallbona de les Monges, Abbess of: Worried about the convent's finances. Restored Yolande of Hungary's tomb. Was addressed as "my lady" and knew a delicious recipe for cookies.

Veciana i Sardà, Josep: Born in Reus. Member of the Academy of Science. The father of two marriageable daughters who sang "Il bacio furtivo" and "La lacrima grossa" with great delicacy.

Villanueva, Jaime: Scholarly friar. Wrote *Viaje literario a las iglesias de España*.

Zurbano: One of the queen's most valiant generals. He and his two sons were shot without trial on January 21, 1845. One of the saddest episodes in nineteenth-century Spanish politics.

A NOTE ON THE TYPE

The text of this book was set on the Linotype in Janson, a typeface thought to have been made by the Dutchman Anton Janson, who was a practicing type founder in Leipzig during the years 1668–1687. However, it has been conclusively demonstrated that these types are actually the work of Nicholas Kis (1650–1702), a Hungarian, who most probably learned his trade from the master Dutch type founder Dirk Voskens. The type is an example of the influential and sturdy Dutch types that prevailed in England up to the time William Caslon developed his own designs from them.

Composed by Maryland Linotype Composition Co., Baltimore, Maryland.
Printed and bound by the Haddon Craftsmen, Scranton, Pennsylvania.
Designed by Iris Weinstein.

Corbit-Calloway Memorial Library
Odessa, Delaware

F PER
Perucho, Juan, 1920-
Natural history

F PER
Perucho, Juan, 1920-
Natural history

TITLE			
DATE DUE	BORROWER'S NAME		ROOM NUMBER
JUL 2 7 1990	346		
AUG. 1 0 1990	346		
APR 2 9 1991	2368		